THE LEGACY

SERIES TITLES

"*The Silver State Stories* by Michael Darcher renders the thwarted souls who work and wager at the Aces Oasis Casino in Reno, Nevada with unstinting insight and a masterful sense of particularity. This collection stands right up there with Denis Johnson's *Jesus' Son*, Greg Sarris' *Grand Avenue*, and Tommy Orange's *There, There*. The writing is that good. After reading *The Silver State Stories*, I'm ready to roll the dice, cash in my chips, (or drown my regret with free drinks) and stumble out into the desert morning."

—PETER DONAHUE
author of *Three Sides Water*

"Michael Darcher delves under the glamour, glitz, and seediness of Nevada to expose the working-class struggles of the souls behind the lights and buzzers, behind the thrills and frills. *The Silver State Stories* are tales of people trying to get by, casino-style, and in their struggles, their schemings, and their successes and failures. Darcher uncovers the true euphoria and desperation of human nature one pull, one roll, one wager at a time."

—MICHAEL CZYZNIEJEWSKI
author of *The Amnesiac in the Maze: Stories*

"Polished, funny, at times unnerving. If you know this world, you're from Reno, where 'No one is happy . . . If we were, we wouldn't be here.' If you don't know this world, reading Darcher's stories will be like learning about your best friend's religion: a little fascination, a little envy, a little 'She did what?' But a great read."

—BARRY KITTERMAN
author of *The Baker's Boy*

THE SILVER STATE STORIES

MICHAEL DARCHER

CORNERSTONE PRESS
UNIVERSITY OF WISCONSIN-STEVENS POINT

Cornerstone Press, Stevens Point, Wisconsin 54481
Copyright © 2024 Michael Darcher
www.uwsp.edu/cornerstone

Printed in the United States of America by
Point Print and Design Studio, Stevens Point, Wisconsin

Library of Congress Control Number: 2024942447
ISBN: 978-1-960329-45-5

Cornerstone Press titles are produced in courses and internships offered by the
Department of English at the University of Wisconsin–Stevens Point.

DIRECTOR & PUBLISHER
Dr. Ross K. Tangedal

EXECUTIVE EDITORS
Jeff Snowbarger, Freesia McKee

EDITORIAL DIRECTOR
Ellie Atkinson

SENIOR EDITORS
Brett Hill, Grace Dahl

PRESS STAFF
Paige Biever, Sam Bjork, Gwen Goetter, Allison Lange, Sophie McPherson,
Holly White, Ava Willett

For Joanne, of course.

And for my brother Ed,
the first to make writing stories seem estimable,
more than that, inherent.

ALSO BY MICHAEL DARCHER:

Odd Comfort (chapbook)

STORIES

. . . towns
of towering blondes, good jazz and booze
the world will never let you have
until the town you came from dies inside.

—Richard Hugo

THIS WRETCHED CONSCIENCE

So much simpler then, the time
spent across the Silver State
table games I viewed through
a bottomless beer glass while

the escape artists grappled
to free themselves from
their real world dreams,
the gamblers their vows of poverty,

the cannibals of love their hearts.
No karma bill was ever served
on my side of the table, no need
for these crocodile hands to rake

my pockets for Susan Bs and
Dwight Ds, the dykes and Ikes
I stowed at home inside
my Crown Royal poke.

No scores to settle, only spreads
to cover and aprons to undo.
Just two sins a dealer might commit,
to be cheap or be needy. I sought

the taut flesh and the sheets
that yielded unlikely shadows
even when we beat the sun to bed.
There was never reflection

in those shaded rooms, each surrender
the mere echo of another's whisper,
the volume knob always in my grasp,
all control remote.

So much simpler then,
when I had myself forgotten.

JACKPOTS ONLY

Once he sees her through the torn screen door, Leonard assumes a smile, enters the trailer without invitation. She is seated, legs crossed, one raised arm holding a white filtered cigarette that sports a Peter Pan collar of red lipstick. She wears a collarless, electric-pink blouse elasticized at every port of entry, a white, plastic belt four inches wide, blue jeans rolled up in pirate cuffs, white go-go boots. Leonard maintains his smile, but he is disappointed that she is still in full make-up, still has her hair done up in a beehive. He had hoped to see a different version of Jackie than the one she displays at the casino.

"You didn't bring any beer?" she says. "I thought 21 dealers made good money."

"I meant to," he says, but it's a lie. A mile away at the Aces Oasis cabaret bar, Alex waits for him with two female tourists and four tickets to the Pointer Sisters cocktail show. Leonard knows what Jackie is expecting, but he plans to stay just long enough to sell her his earrings. "I didn't know what brand you drink," he says. This deal is strictly cash and dash.

"I don't have a brand. I take whatever fits." She lights another cigarette but leaves the room without it.

Leonard surveys the trailer, surprised at how cavernous it seems. He studies each furnishing: the pine-board veneer that serves as wallpaper, the twin couches both deeply soiled, a shriveled aloe plant, brass elephant head bookends that hold no books, a shadeless lamp, an empty wooden coffee table painted shiny red, a paint-splattered magazine rack full of torn, dated fan club magazines. Most of all, he notices the DayGlo velveteen picture of Cher that hangs above the console. Adorned in a fringed cowhide blouse and a beaded headband, Cher sits in a canoe, arms crossed and lips parted in delicious privity, suggesting to him she has a secret she just might divulge.

Leonard checks his watch. Where is she? He drags the red table over to a couch wondering why every piece of furniture has been pushed against a wall. He unhinges the elk horn clips of his leather case and lets it unfold. He holds it at arm's length like a calendar, then jostles the case until the dozen sets of earrings hang untangled. He sets the display in the center of the table. He studies each pair, wonders which ones she will buy.

THE EARRINGS WEREN'T HIS IDEA. It was his sister who came home wearing the Jock Scott he had abandoned after inadvertently clipping the barb. "This is too cool," she said. Her friends thought so too, and offered to pay Leonard for his creations although some of them, the punks, asked him not to clip the barbs. A crafts show jeweler also found his flies "conceptual." That winter, he tied a thousand flies that would never find water. By Memorial Day, he had made enough money to leave Manchester.

His plan was to fish the California Sierra, then the blue ribbons up in Montana, but a blown piston rod and a bad run of cards in Reno forced him to get a job in the slot department at the Aces Oasis. The indifference his earrings received surprised him, but only briefly. The Blue Duns and Bitch Creek Nymphs, flies he had brought with him from New Hampshire, didn't sell well in the casino so he created garish, fictitious flies that did. These new earrings became the rage among the cocktail hostesses and women dealers, one of whom pulled strings to get him into a dealing school in return for three pairs.

After class at the bar, he boasted to the three other guys in his 21 training school, who were keenly aware of the attention Leonard received, that it took a new fly to hook a new fish. What Leonard didn't tell them was that these women who had initially regarded him as moody and odd now found him sensitive and smart. In their eyes, Leonard was an artist. Best of all, the earrings became the pick-up lines he had never mastered at Dartmouth. Now Leonard always keeps a pair on his person. In his sports coat lies a pair of feathered beauties he'll use tonight to reel in his half of the tourists.

"HERE YOU GO, CASH DADDY," Jackie says and thrusts a Coors at him, keeping the Schlitz for herself. She places a bowl of stick pretzels on the coffee table and sits beside him, closer than she has to. "Fab!" she says and plucks free the pair he thinks are the most tawdry.

He knows he is staring at her excessive make-up, knows that she knows, but still he cannot avert his eyes from her eyeshadow. The iridescence reminds him of fish scales. In her, he sees the eyes of an old, tired stockie that has somehow survived, become indigenous. He guesses that she is a good five years older than him, thirty, maybe thirty-one.

"Do you fish?"

"No," she says. "I don't like being near water."

Leonard tries a different cast. "Have you lived here long?"

"Six months. Is that long?"

"This is only the second mobile home I've ever been in," he tells her. "The first one was an office on a used car lot. I liked the car but I didn't like the salesman, so I didn't buy the car."

She looks at him then drops the earrings to the display. She selects another pair and holds them up to the light. "How much did you say these cost?"

Her eyeshadow is the color of an Earl Scheib paint job his parents once got on the family Ford. "Still $29.95," he says, three times their actual price. She lets this pair as well plummet to the case.

THIS AFTERNOON, LEONARD was in the casino to sell a pair to a day shift roulette dealer and to visit with a friend in the slot department he hadn't seen since he'd jumped to swing shift and begun dealing cards. Jackie wasn't someone he'd planned on seeing. They hadn't worked together. And he usually avoided women who were taller than him.

"What's in the case?" she asked as she made her way down the aisle to a woman seated on a stool between two slot machines. Leonard felt foolish trailing her. He hoped none of the nearby day shift dealers were watching.

"This one's jammed," the woman on the stool said, pointing to one slot machine while feeding quarters into another.

"Guess what?" Jackie said. She motioned for Leonard to open his case. "This is the last day I'll ever have to sell coin rolls out of this stupid apron. Starting tomorrow, I'll just be paying off jackpots and doing the dinky repair stuff on the machines. No more old broads poking me in the ribs when they want change. Starting tomorrow, I'm jackpots only."

She fiddled momentarily with the coin slot. "You've jammed the machine," she told the woman. "I'll have to call a JPO."

"Why can't you fix it?"

"If I could, I would," Jackie said and then remembered. "Tomorrow, I will be able to fix it."

"That won't do," the woman said. "We're leaving tomorrow."

"Then you got a problem," Jackie said. The woman's good machine paid out ten quarters.

"Cherries, always cherries," the woman said. "I hate cherries."

"You got two problems," Jackie said and turned to examine Leonard's earrings, and again, he thought, pushed herself into him.

"Come here," she ordered as she walked by two service lights, past two surprised customers who would have to buy their rolls of quarters from someone else.

Leonard slowed down when he saw that she was leading him to Lois, her roommate. He stopped altogether when he saw the roulette dealer's disparaging look. He heard Jackie calling his name. He sighed hard and stared down the dealer. She had no right to be offended. It was the slot department who had to bear the brunt of Jackie and Lois's oddity. As a slot floorman, he'd heard the others laugh at Lois's acrylic blonde wig, her make-up, the way she wore her change apron slung below her gut like a bandido. He had heard the cashiers express their disbelief that someone her size would wear stretch pants. "Miss Piggy" they called her. He sensed that they disliked Jackie even more because they knew that despite the capri pants, the stiletto heels, the beehive hair-do, she was still an attraction, and it was only a matter of time until she advanced to a better job in another department.

"Show Lois," Jackie said. Ceremoniously, he opened the jaws of the jewelry case that contained three sets of earrings.

"Yeah, so?" Lois said.

"I think they're fab," Jackie said. "I want a pair."

"I don't," Lois said and walked away.

"I do," Jackie said. She shut her eyes for a full second, enough time for Leonard to compare her green eyeshadow with her red lipstick. Merry Christmas, he thought.

"The money's at my house," she said.

Leonard smiled. He could interpret that line. He laughed and dismissed the notion, but afterward, he went home and crafted eight new pairs.

HE CANNOT HEAR THE WIND, but from his seat in the living room, Leonard feels it, sees it pressing into the trailer walls. He wonders now if it's the wind that has pushed each piece of furniture, like a tumbleweed against the wall where it can go no further. "I feel like I'm being digested," he says.

She sits stiffly, gazing not at him but at velveteen Cher over his shoulder.

"The wind. This trailer. This room. It's churning."

"What are you talking about?" she says.

He shakes his beer can, wishes it was empty. "Doesn't living in a trailer get to you?"

"Everything gets to me after a while."

"How many rooms are there anyway?"

"Four, if you count all this as one room and don't count the bathroom."

"That's it," he says. "Four rooms, four stomachs. We're inside a cow. We're nothing but cud."

Jackie raises a penciled eyebrow. She looks at Leonard with concern.

"Have you ever milked a cow?" he asks.

"What's that supposed to mean?"

"Didn't you grow up on a farm?" It's just a guess.

"Yeah," she says. "A funny farm."

"Aren't you from Modesto or Bakersfield or some place like that?"

"I don't remember."

"I had an ant farm once," he says. "But all the ants died. I put new ants in but they died, too. They all crawled to the bottom and died. It took me a week to shake them through the passages and get them all to the top. It was like owning a labyrinth. I used to feel that way about our slot section. Luck runs through the casino like a Minotaur, don't you think?"

Jackie extends the same raised eyebrow. "I'm going to take a piss," she says.

Make sure you put it back, he wants to tell her but fears she won't see the humor in that either. He checks his watch, knowing by now Alex and the two women are standing in line for the show and wondering where he is. He knows he could drain his beer, gather his valise and be out the door before she returns, but he doesn't. There's unfinished business here, he realizes, and it's not just the earrings.

He eyes the DayGlo Cher and sinks further into the couch. Jackie isn't like the women dealers. With her, his elliptical words and seductive earrings have been nothing but bullets fired into the sky. It's situations, Leonard knows, not people, that he's learned to master. Recognize desire and offer it as bait. His earrings have taught him that. But tonight, inside this mobile home, there's nothing familiar. And that's the allure.

Leonard twirls a set of earrings, lets them drop to the table like he saw her do. He shakes his display, seeing how many sets he can snarl. His choice is simple. He can fish from his usual spot and catch nothing. Or he can toss all his flies in the river and jump in after them, letting the river, her river, carry him downstream and wash him onto another bank, to the one place where he just might limit out.

Leonard chooses Plan B.

And thinks Leonard: I'll see this woman exposed. I'll make her eyes turn all new shades of green. I'll know her.

SHE RETURNS WITH A BOTTLE of Bud and a can of Hamm's.

"You really don't have a brand, do you?"

"I don't have time to look," she says. "What's the difference? I got them free. You get them free. What are you, a beer snob?"

He avoids her eyes. He counts the sets of earrings inside the valise, studies the ones he made just for her. "Where's Lois tonight?"

"At work, I hope. It's too quiet. Do you like music?"

"Are the Kennedys gun-shy?"

She walks past him to the console unable, or unwilling he thinks, to respond to his glibness. Fair enough. It's supposed to be her show anyway, not his.

When she faces him, holding out record albums as if they were steering wheels, studying their titles with no concern about scratching or smudging them, Leonard feels that he is being offered something. He notices that she has removed her rouge and eye shadow. The eyelashes and lipstick remain, but the absence of other coloring makes her look younger. He watches her stack four albums on the spool. He hears the control arm slide over the top LP. The first album drops. He is surprised how unscratched this version of "Half-Breed" sounds.

"You really like Cher, don't you?"

"I adore her," she says and picks a new set of earrings to finger. "I named my daughter after hers. Wouldn't it be neat if they became friends someday?"

"You have a daughter?"

Jackie nods solemnly. "Chastity. She's six."

"She's not here, is she?"

"No." She draws a cigarette from a red vinyl case. She murmurs the lyrics as she lights up.

"Why Cher?"

"I love her hair," Jackie says and strokes her own. "I love her nose, those teeth, everything about her. I admire her taste in younger men. I really like the way she dresses. It's cool. Before Chastity, I used to dress like that."

"Why?"

She impales him with a look. "Why does anybody do anything? The way I see it, those who got it, show it. Those who don't, hide it." She pulls at her sleeves. Leonard sees the lines on her arms that the elastic has made.

He tries to guess when this album was first released. He wonders what the appeal was, tries to imagine what a Cher concert was like, wonders who went, what they looked like, what the original fans took for a buzz. "You're an anachronism," he tells her.

She blows out distasteful smoke. "I have no idea what you're talking about," she says. "I'm not that complicated."

He swallows half his beer and asks her to dance. She offers him her erect arm then draws him slowly to her. She wants to lead and he lets her. He hated it in the seventh grade, but tonight it feels good to dance with someone taller. They dance in a slow, continuous circle. He likes it that her perfume smells like Jello. It no longer matters that she is different from the others. What matters is that she is different from him.

They dance through the silence between songs. They swirl slowly, cheek to cheek, chest to chest, right into "I Got You, Babe." She does not recoil when he kisses her ear.

"If only I could get a dealing job," she says. "If I can make some money, show them I can hold a job, then maybe I can get my daughter back."

"Who's got your daughter?"

"The state."

He doesn't ask which one. "Where's your husband?" he asks instead.

"How would I know? I never had one." She stops dancing.

"Sorry. I meant the father."

She fishes for a cigarette.

"So where's the father?"

"How the hell should I know?" she says and goes for her can of beer. "He could still be in this town for all I know. Does it matter?" She looks at her cigarette, at the earrings, at him. "This beer sucks," she says. "I'm getting another."

Leonard sits down in his same spot. He rests his feet on the coffee table and shakes his display. He notices that one pair is missing.

THE ENTIRE SIDE OF AN ALBUM plays before she returns. She is now dressed in a pink, fluffy bathrobe and carries with her two jelly jars full of wine. He thinks that she's been crying. A single strand of stiff, lacquered hair hangs free from her beehive. He sees that she has removed more make-up, and it occurs to him that he is witnessing some sort of reverse metamorphosis, a time lapse film being rewound, a video in which the butterfly forsakes its luster and returns to the cocoon. Now she looks his age, a disturbing thought.

"Dance with me," he says but she wants to wait for a fast song. She is chain smoking.

Leonard drinks, shudders. "What is this?"

"MD 20/20. I'm out of beer."

He sets down the jar, picks up the valise. "Pick a pair," he says. "Try them on."

Without hesitation, she pulls a pair of Adult Damsels and hooks them both to one ear.

"Good. You needed color."

"I got color," she says. "I got three tattoos. All cherries. I went out and got them when I found out about Cher's tattoos."

He braces himself, then swallows more wine. "Show me," he says.

"This'll do," she says and stands up to a new song.

So does Leonard. La da da de dee. She gyrates in a succession of dances, calling out the name of each one: the Fish, the Hully Gully, the Boogaloo, the Skate, the Shake. He tries to mimic her. La da da de dah. As soon as he does, she switches to a new dance.

It's the last song on the last album and the silence that follows seems to bother her. She shakes when lighting a filterless cigarette from a fresh pack.

"God damn it," she says. "He never should have left."

"Who?"

She looks at him angrily. "Sonny."

"How do you know it was his idea?"

"How do I know?" She walks over to the magazine rack and grabs a handful of magazines. Each one that she throws at him has Cher on the cover. "I know," she says. "Besides, it's always the guy."

Leonard drinks the last of his Mogen David and goes to the kitchen to pour himself another. He hears footsteps and braces, thinks that Jackie, enraged, is coming after him. He turns but she is nowhere.

He stares at his own reflection in the kitchen window. He laughs at his fear. Does she want him to be her guy? He hears the wind and looks outside for evidence, but sees no trembling leaves, no raised dust, no tumbleweeds. There are no signs of weather except the sound. Again, he catches his reflection. He wonders if Alex and the tourist women will dance the Hully Gully tonight.

GONE NOW ARE ALL VESTIGES OF MAKE-UP. She has removed her eyelashes and, Leonard notices, his earrings. She has let down her hair. Stiff and straight, it falls down to her waist. Thick bangs now cover her forehead, reaching almost to her eyebrows. In a small way, she does remind him of Cher.

"Show me your tattoos."

She walks out of the kitchen to the console to play a new stack of records. She brings back her jar and her cigarettes.

"Show me."

"I'll show you one," she says without affection. She separates the top of her robe, revealing her right areola which has been colored blood-red and given a cherry rump and a green stem that curls toward her sternum.

Leonard reaches to touch it.

"No," she says and covers herself.

He recognizes the music. "Dance?" he asks at the next slow song.

"They used to drive his and her pink Mustangs," she says. "They used to do everything together."

In her arms, under her lead, again he finds contentment. They dance and linger in embrace after song's end. This time, it's Leonard who breaks free. He flashes her his biggest set of dolphin eyes. She pauses only to grab a fresh pack of cigarettes before allowing herself to be led down the hallway. "This one," she says at the second door and closes it behind them.

In the dull moonlight, his eyes never leave her. She's got Cher's teeth, he thinks. And her hair, though he wishes that she'd kept it up in a beehive because now she looks like other women. He wants to ask her about Sonny. He wants to learn why any man would leave Cher, but he doesn't. He's afraid she'll see the Sonny in him.

He knows his hands are ice so he is careful where he puts them. Her hair feels fake. Doll's hair. He draws her closer. Her hair feels strange, but her kisses stranger. Limp, exaggerated, offered in amateur passion.

"How old are you?" he asks.

"Twenty-one."

"Blackjack," he says. When she doesn't respond, he kisses her and tastes cigarette smoke.

"Jackie can't be your real name."

"It's Jack. Nice name to give to a girl, huh? I think my parents wanted a boy."

"It could have been worse," he says. "In China, they toss female babies into the gutter like trout heads, or else torture and maim them for life by boxing their feet. At least they did until the Boxer Rebellion."

He hears her sigh and realizes he's doing it again, trolling his stream, not hers. So he makes his move.

He is refused. She is willing to kiss and be held but not caressed, and after his third wave of passion defeats him with a single "Please" before rolling away to her edge of the bed.

"Fabulous," Leonard mutters. He props himself against the headboard and tries to catch a glimpse of her face. He looks for a flaw in her complexion, a birthmark, a blemish, anything that will make her less winning. But the absence of light and color cleanses her. Eyes closed, she is innocent. Pure. His anger dissipates. He wonders how many more years her pillow will erase from her face, wonders how complete her metamorphosis will be.

He scans the room for a clock, knowing it's too late to make the Pointer Sisters show. He thinks about leaving anyway, but remembers he hasn't collected for the earrings. He can get that much at least. "Jackie," he whispers, but she is fast asleep.

HE IS ALMOST ASLEEP WHEN he hears a door being slammed. A second slam brings him upright. He remembers where he is and for a horrifying moment, wonders if Chastity's father is the one making all the noise. He stares at Jackie who is asleep, wonders if he'll fight for her honor. He watches her thread her fingers, prayer-like. If she has heard anything, she does not let on.

A third slam and now the whole trailer shakes.

The fourth slam is softer, muted. It sounds like someone knocking on their door.

"Who's there?" Leonard asks. He looks at Jackie for help. "Who's there?" he asks again before a more horrifying thought seizes him. Perhaps it's Lois, drunk and amorous, preparing to join them. He grips the top of the covers. He has often dreamed of a ménage à trois. But not this one. Not tonight.

He hopes whoever is out there will go away but the next slam, coming a minute later, is the loudest yet.

"Who's there?" he asks.

The next slam, louder still, rouses him out of bed. He kicks around the rug but can't find his pants.

Another slam.

"Screw it," he says and bounds into the hallway. Through the gauzy light extending from the kitchen window, he spots a white plastic belt on the hallway floor. He wraps the perforated end around his palm. He notices that the front door is open.

"Who's out there?" he asks, swinging the belt like a sling. "Who's there?" he shouts, leaping into the kitchen.

No one is there. Not under the kitchen table, not in the front closet, not kneeling behind the console. Leonard walks up to the open door. He peers out at the starless sky, at the rows of unlit condos that loom above the trailer park. "Who's there?" he wants to know.

He locks the door, walks to the bathroom. Unwilling to let go of the belt, he uses his left hand to pee, stares into the mirror imagining his own tattoos. He envisions a stack of one hundred dollar chips needled into his breast. Or an ace and a face *the queen of hearts?* etched on his bicep. Maybe a pair of rolling dice tumbling across his knuckles. He swings the bathroom door out of his way. Boldly, he opens the door to the first bedroom and peers in.

There is nothing in there that belongs to Lois. No bed. No bureau or piles of cast off clothes. The room is empty except for a hair dryer, the dome and seat type he's seen in beauty parlors.

He tiptoes down to the only other door. He hesitates, then opens it, but all he finds is a cement basin and a washer and dryer. He retreats to the living room and feels the front of both couches. Neither one is a sleeper.

When he returns to her room, the light is on and Jackie is awake, smoking a cigarette.

"Was that you?" she asks.

"No."

"What's with the belt?" she asks but he won't tell her.

"You got scared, didn't you?" she says and laughs smoke.

"No. Yes."

"What are you so scared of?"

"I don't know," he says and fumbles to unravel the belt. "I thought there was someone out there."

"There probably was."

He wonders if he is safer in or out of bed.

"You're afraid of the dark," she says on her way out of the room. "That's sweet."

I know your secret, he thinks, but the realization offers him no comfort. It pushes into him like the wind he can feel prodding the trailer walls.

When she returns, he sees a second tattoo. It lies on the inside of her left thigh. It, too, is a cherry of equal size to the first. "Cherries, always cherries," he says.

She draws herself to him and allows his hands full range of her. He is pleased that she does not shrink when reaching past him for the light.

"Can we leave it on?" he asks.

"Cool!" she says and keeps saying the word as if to remind herself.

Her distraction does not deter him. His hands touch everywhere, especially her tattoos. He is disappointed that the dyed skin feels no different. Still, his hands light on the cherries like bees, then trace other parts of her, rapt, impatient, always returning to the cherries.

"Slow down," she says. "It's all right here."

Leonard obeys. He does not tell her he is searching for the third tattoo.

LEONARD WAKES UP ALONE. Beyond the closed door, he hears running water, raised voices, smells coffee. He kneels on the bed and looks out the window for evidence of wind. Nothing shimmers. He dresses and for laughs, fastens the white belt around his waist.

At the kitchen table, Lois stares into a make-up mirror and applies mascara to newly fastened eyelashes. Across the table, Jackie primps in front of her own mirror. She dabs at her eyelids with a finger of iridescent goo. Her face is thick with make-up. Her hair is loosely stacked. Leonard removes the white belt. Only Lois notices.

"Morning," he says and sits in the chair between them. Lois moves away her mirror and chair.

"Thanks," Leonard says, grateful for the room. Lois glares and moves away even further.

"Would you like some coffee?" Jackie asks.

"Yes, please," and then, "I'll get it," when Jackie makes no attempt to serve him.

From the kitchen, he hears Lois say, "That's him? That makes me feel even worse." He watches Jackie light two cigarettes and hand Lois one.

"You'll get over it," she tells Lois. "You always do."

"But why do you have to wave it in my face?" Lois asks. "Why can't you ever go over to their place?"

"I told you on Day One," Jackie says. "I'm a gypsy. I'm a tramp. I'm a thief. Help me with my hair, will you?"

He absorbs Lois's stare when she rises and stands behind Jackie, watches her caress Jackie's shoulders. "Do you think I like taking a taxi home?" he hears Lois ask. "You think I like sleeping in someone else's car?"

"You could have slept on the couch," Jackie says.

"And listen all night to you and someone else? No thanks."

He thinks about leaving but decides that would be something the old Leonard, not the Plan B Leonard would do, so he returns to the table with a full cup of coffee and endures Lois's disapproval. For thirty-five minutes, he drinks instant coffee and watches them pin, pluck, smear, curl, comb, dab, gloss, spray, spritz, and pat until they are butterflies again. Until they are what he and everyone else at the casino are used to seeing, expect to see, and Leonard realizes that he has been waiting to witness their return all along. That until this moment, he has been trespassing. Poaching.

"Do me," he says.

"What?"

"Make me over," he says to Jackie. "I need color, too."

It's Lois who slides over her make-up tray and begins applying foundation in steady swipes. Leonard can detect no pattern in her application. Each dab seems intentionally arbitrary and although he thinks she is having fun at his expense, he lets her apply a round of blush. He closes his eyes, which Lois immediately goes after with fingers of eyeshadow, and imagines himself a rainbow trout nestled in cool morning mud. When he opens his eyes, Lois stops, puts everything away. Leonard beams and feels the crevices his smile has just made. He looks to Jackie for approval, but she is in the kitchen hunched over a bowl of cold cereal and a magazine. She has been there all along.

He stands beside her until she has no choice but to look. "What do you think?" he asks.

"I *don't* think," she says, emptying the box of cereal onto the countertop. "I don't think you should be here." She passes her hand through the mound of flakes, searching vainly for the prize.

Leonard goes for his sports jacket and valise that one of them has placed by the door. He wants to open the case to see how many pairs are missing. Instead, he asks, "How many sets did you decide to take?"

Jackie and Lois laugh at this. Lois points to the living room. To Cher. Jackie stands and tugs at her blouse. She checks her contours in a mirror.

"You look nice," Lois says.

"I feel great," Jackie says.

"What about my earrings?" Leonard says.

"No more change apron," Jackie says. "Starting today, I, Jackie Pratt, am jackpots only. Yes!"

Door open, he waves to her in small swipes, then to Lois, then to Cher, who he notices is wearing a Damsel in her right ear.

In the sunlight, the condos seem more distant. Slowly, he backs out of the driveway careful not to raise any dust. He wants to leave it all untouched, leave no evidence of himself.

Catch and release. He avoids catching his reflection in the rearview mirror, but he can't avoid the reek that's new to his upholstery so he yields to it. He inhales raspberry Jello, deeply this time, and thinks about going fishing. He decides that when he gets home, he'll tie as many flies as are missing from his valise. Real flies that will catch real fish. Then he'll wash his face, locate his fishing license and a fly rod, and walk down to the Truckee River. He needs to be near water.

SUITS AND BODIES

I killed them at the interview. Had an answer for every question they asked—but I'm hardly bragging. It was the stock stuff everyone asks.

"Why do you want to be a floorman?"

"What qualities do you have that would make you a good pit administrator?"

"What would *you* do to improve the Aces Oasis?"

Batting practice. Even when they asked if I'd have a problem writing up any of my former crewmates. I told them what they wanted to hear, that I understood putting on a suit was crossing a line, that my fidelity lay with the company, not the dealers. The only question I snagged on was when DeLuca asked, "What do you consider to be your weaknesses?"

Like any good poker player, I paused for the same interval before responding. But inside, I was scrambling to manufacture something believable because the truth is: I don't think in those terms. The world is lousy with people, and DeLuca is probably one of them, who beat themselves up on a daily basis. I don't.

What I wanted to say was, "My ability to humor tit-heads like you." What I said was, "My temporary inexperience."

AT HOME, WHILE RUNNING A DAB of gel through my hair, I wondered who among my crewmates I would write up if the pit bulls pushed it on me. It's common practice, management asking a new floorman to write up a former crewmate as a show of good faith. A reminder that you're now a suit.

My crew thinks I'm on glue for putting in for one of the three floorman positions the company listed a week ago. Dead Bob, who rarely initiates conversation, asked me in the middle of a thirty-minute hand while four pit bosses lurked over us like crows, "So what are you going to do: work or watch other people work?" After things died down, Max said something like, "I always thought the floor was for people who can't deal." And Liz, who's new to the crew, mustered up enough moxie to tell me that I dress too well to be a floorman.

I'm wondering about it too. I tell my friends in the other forty-nine that dealing high-limit craps for a good store like the Aces Oasis is a drunkard's dream. And for my metabolism, it is. I haven't used an alarm clock in three years. When I wake up is when my day begins. I sleep like a saint except for when Hoppy and Nick bring by some powder or pill that's got a little hidden zip in it. Like last night. Nick claimed the stuff had just a trace of meth in it, but it turned me into a lighthouse for a good six hours.

People are amazed that I can live next to an ambulance service. But I never hear them—Max claims it's because I don't have a conscience—so they're not a nuisance. And rent is cheap. The house stood empty for three months before I rented it for a hundred less than what the owner wanted. And I got to meet Hoppy and Nick, the graveyard EMTs, who provide what little uncertainty exists in my life. That's the real reason for putting in for the floor. It's not that dealing is so bad. I just want to try something new.

EVERYONE SEEMS TO BE badgering me this week. The dry cleaner says I only gave her four white shirts. Ernie the Pencil, the swing shift schedule maker, is harassing me to accept six-day work weeks like everyone else until Labor Day. The landlord wants to raise my rent—I shouldn't have bragged. And Nick and Hoppy want me to ride with them in the ambulance.

"It's a whole 'nother world," Hoppy said last night when he showed me the four different colored pills in his palm, his latest victim score.

"Yeah, the underworld," I said. What was in his hand looked like M&Ms.

"You chicken?" Nick asked. At first, I thought he meant the pills.

THE THING I LIKE BEST ABOUT working on the 4-C craps crew is that no one seems anxious to burden me with their private lives. I hate it when someone reveals something personal because I know they're doing it for a reason. I'm not a priest. I can't offer absolution, and on the 4-C crew, I don't have to. There's no line leading to the confessional. Conversation with Dead Bob is like pulling teeth. Liz doesn't fraternize with dealers. Just Born Jimmy has a new girlfriend so as soon as the shift ends, he's out the door getting his wick wet. Unless he's hammered, Number One just talks shop. Only Max has ever felt the need to confide, usually about his bad luck with men.

And the only reason I've feigned interest is that Max isn't telling me; he's just telling someone hetero. I think it's important to him that some testosterone jockey like me tolerates him. Still, every time he begins a story about his latest heartbreak, there's this naked moment when we catch each other's eye and realize again, this is for his sake only. That it's acceptance, not understanding, he wants. Even so, I realized in the shower today that if the pit office demanded it, Max is the only dealer I'd have qualms writing up.

I'M NOT HOME FIVE MINUTES when Hoppy and Nick are at my door.

"Have we got a surprise for you," Nick says.

I know they want me to guess but I'm not in the mood. "Beers are still in the refrigerator," I tell them.

"So when's the last time you had hash?" Hoppy says and shows me a wrinkled aluminum ball the size of a lima bean.

"You guys." My anticipation betrays me. I put on my sweats in front of them and don't feel faggy about it.

I assume my normal spot in my La-Z-Boy. Hoppy is busy cramming hash into the bowl of a foldaway wooden pipe. "You took his pipe too?" Hoppy and Nick laugh at this. I reach for a beer that one of them has brought out from the kitchen. With my free hand, I wag a finger. "Someday."

"No way," Nick says.

"It's a perf plan," Hoppy says. "Who's going to rat us out?"

"It's the only reason I come to work," Nick says. "To find out what's on today's menu."

"Doesn't it affect your work?" Stupid question.

"Exactly," Nick says.

The second time Hoppy packs the pipe, we strike a deal. They take me for a ride and I teach them craps.

IT'S ALL I CAN DO NOT TO take the paddle that covers the slot to the drop box and shove it down DeLuca's gullet. Each time he does something on the game, like examine the dice, or write up a fill slip, or extend a player a marker, he turns my way to show me what he's doing. He's already treating me like a suit.

I avoid him as best I can. I keep my eyes riveted to the layout, to the bets on the table. I avoid my crewmates' silent attention, most of all Dead Bob's amusement. Everyone assumes I've decided.

THEY ACTUALLY HANDED OUT diplomas when we completed craps school. And because I was ranked first, I was immediately promoted to the pit. When I called my father to tell him I was now a dealer, he thought I meant pusher. "What were you before?" he asked. "A pimp?"

TONIGHT SUCKED. We dumped our game big time, to the tune of eighty grand, which brought all kinds of heat on the game. DeLuca changed the dice three times, like they were dirty diapers. Herrera kept badgering Liz to pick up the pace. Even the casino manager parked his carcass on the game for fifteen minutes, as if his presence alone would staunch the bleeding. It didn't happen. Worst of all, the players were as tight as virgins. An eighty thousand dollar hit for five hundred in tips. Thanks, you lucky stiffs.

Afterwards, Number One and Liz, surprisingly, wanted to talk shop at the bar, but I wasn't in the mood. I walked out with Max who was on his way to a date with some guy he met at his step aerobics class. I told him he seemed happy.

A year ago, he wasn't. I don't know the circumstances, but I know he wanted out. He was unsure whether to move to

Florida, to quit the club and start an export business, so he threw the I-Ching. Typical Max. Willing to place his faith in what three coins might tell him.

Number One had a field day with this. "What next? The Ouija board? Tea leaves? Dionne Warwick?" When Max turned to me, I asked him what was the worst thing that could happen.

"I could always come back here," he said. "But I'd rather die."

Number One softened, asked Max how much Spanish he knew, if he was willing to play macho. "No offense," he said, "but communism is the only alternative lifestyle down there."

Dead Bob had one question. "Why do you need *three* coins?"

IT SOUNDS FUNNY, BUT I MET Nick and Hoppy by accident. When they showed up at my door in their white jumpsuits with their names ascribed in red cursive stitching on their breast pockets, I assumed they were pest control sprayers or some service like that. It wouldn't have been the first time the landlord sent someone over without notifying me. Then I saw the Ambulance Service patches on their sleeves and backs.

"You're blocking us," the one named Nick said.

He read my confusion as if diagnosing an emergency. "Your car. It's blocking our driveway."

"You're killing our commission," the smaller tech, Hopkins, said. "Move your Mustang. Pronto, Tonto."

Initially, they declined my offer of a beer, but an hour later, they were back, off shift, ready to accept my liquid apology and to offer me a hit of what looked like MDA.

MAX IS RIGHT. I DON'T have a conscience. But he is wrong to assume that a conscience is worth having. All a conscience provides is another chance to feel crummy. It's all a drill bit driven by the biggest fear of all: someone else's discovery of the real you. What I have is a responsibility to myself. When I show Jimmy or Liz a new way to pay off a bet, or how to inform a tourist of a winning bet before some other flea claims it, I'm not acting out of conscience. I'm acting out of self-interest. The sooner Jimmy and Liz learn to deal the high-limit game, the sooner I get to quit babysitting. Informing a player about a sleeper bet prevents a gung-ho observation goon from getting me written up for lax game security. That's one reason why I'm reluctant to put on a suit. Corporate fidelity? Dream on, DeLuca. The only allegiance I have is to myself.

THE SECOND TIME HOPPY AND NICK came over, they told me about their scam. I've heard about the parking valets taking somebody's 'Vette for a ride on Route 80 before bringing it to the door. And maids who swipe guests' contraband, knowing there will be no formal complaint. And cocktail hostesses who get hard-ons to leave by serving up specials, Visine-laced drinks guaranteed to give any pest the screaming squirts within fifteen minutes. But Nick and Hoppy's plan is a beaut. Whenever an accident victim fits their M.O., Nick goes for the gurney and trauma box while Hoppy stabilizes the victim and gets in his ear, tells him that he knows there are drugs somewhere, that the cops are on their way, that if the lucky bastard tells him where his stash is, he will dispose it for him.

"And they believe you?" I asked.

"Hoppy plays a good good cop," Nick said.

"I suppose you guys are making money off this."

"No jackpots yet," Nick said. "Maybe an ounce of bud. Or a gram of crank."

"Don't forget the crack," Hoppy said.

That got a laugh out of Nick. "Fifty rocks. A big pile of albino rabbit turds. We tossed them out. Nasty stuff."

"Didn't you expect the guy to come back for his stash?"

Both of them flashed me a *New to this country?* look. "That would be a little piggy," Nick said. "Besides, they think we're doing them a favor."

"Symbiotic relationship," Hoppy said and told me about his dream of attending pharmacy school.

ON OUR WAY TO HIS ECLIPSE, Max, insistent that I check out his new sports car, tells me that he was once married. In front of his sleek new ride, so shiny I can see my own reflection in the black gloss paint, Max admits that he had fought off what he calls *my tendencies* for as long as he could, until the idea of sex with his wife physically repulsed him.

"Was she that ugly?"

"She was stunning," he says. I find myself unable to disengage from Max's gaze, a look that, for once, measures me fully. Once again, he wants from me something I don't have.

I'm no homophobe, Max knows that now. The first time he came out to me, I said great, more women for me, which wasn't the response he wanted. So I told him that life is too short not to be happy, something I've repeated several times since, usually during his latest crisis. But as I catch my reflection in the polished hood that has yet to receive its first scratch, I realize that I'm telling a lie. Not the gay part. The happy part. No one in Reno is happy. If we were, we wouldn't be here.

Leaning against the car, staring out at the skyline, Max seems a light year beyond.

"Max. Max."

"Leaving her isn't what I regret," he says. "Or hurting her. I just wish I hadn't waited for her to make the recognition."

"What makes you think it would have been any better coming from you?"

Max ponders this which provides me an out. "Nice car," I say. "When you die, can I have it?" I dig out my keys though I'm two blocks away from my truck. I hope that Hoppy and Nick are working tonight, that they'll bring over a bushel of sudden happiness. "You got yourself a real Batmobile here," I tell Max and pat him on the back. "Now go find yourself a Boy Wonder."

BECAUSE HE BELIEVES THERE is a reason for everything, my father, Controller of TechnoComp, finds gambling pointless. The notion that a bluff might subvert the winning hand is unfathomable. Twenty-two black? Box cars? To someone who has held the same job for sixteen years, chance is not an attraction but an onus.

POWDERS ARE THE WORST. Hoppy has a pharmaceutical book with a picture and description of every pill ever produced in the free world so there's minimal risk there. And of course, anything organic is recognizable. So are the garage drugs, which I won't do. But powder is another story and one with a perpetual new ending. Nick still bristles about the time Hoppy took a quick snoot of what turned to be PCP and almost ended up taking a ride in his own ambulance. It's Nick's job to identify the narcotic in the powder. Anything he can't identify with a dab and a taste, he condemns.

"I don't know what these wahoos are putting in this stuff," Nick will say. "There's no quality control anymore."

ESSEX ISN'T MY REAL NAME, but I won't say what is. Why should I tell you something that my own crew doesn't know? No one here outside of Personnel knows my given name, and I'm not about to tell them.

The need for distance is something I learned my first week dealing when, after reprimanding a player for claiming another player's bet, I was pulled off the game and chastised for my poor customer relations. When I tried to explain that I was providing game security as I was taught to do in craps school, the pit boss laughed. "Who do you think you are?" he asked. "Brinks? The only thing you or me or anyone here has to offer is service. That's the only thing we provide. You want security? Then go secure a name tag."

At the bar that night, I made this vow: they get my skills, but they don't get me. Not even my name. I marched up to Wardrobe. I had the woman print out ESSEX, my home-town street, on a name tag. The name meant nothing to her. The only thing she wanted to know was how to spell it.

At work, that's who I am. Essex. It's all an act anyway, being polite to customers you'd just as soon jab with a fork as pay off their bets. I don't want these fleas calling me by my real name, assuming a false familiarity when the only reason either of us is here is that we want each other's money.

THE OTHER DEALERS ARE STARTING to lay it on thick. Number One now calls me Benedict Essex. Liz, who has been on our crew less than two months, calls me Yoko, says this is tantamount to the break-up of the Beatles. In the toke room in front of ten other dealers, One Can Nan says a part of swing shift will die if I put on a suit. Radar doesn't say anything. Instead, he shadows me, arms folded, in exaggerated pit boss poses.

I tell them that I haven't decided yet. And I haven't. But my consideration alone condemns me. Screw 'em. If I go, I'll write them all up.

WHILE WAITING FOR THE TOKE committee to divvy up tonight's tips, I draw up a P and M list on a cocktail napkin. I'd prefer to use my palm, but the pen I borrowed is a felt tip. I list the minuses first.

> *Drop in pay*
> *Cost of new clothes*
> *Numbing shop talk with stiffs like DeLuca*
> *Eventual boredom*
> *Will miss the game*

I add to this last entry: *- not the crew, the game*
Next, my plus list:

> *Something new*
> *Rise in the ranks*
> *More money eventually*
> *Prove Dad wrong*

I stare at this column long enough to miss Max's offer to buy a round. The brevity of both lists bothers me. I ball up the napkin and throw it at Liz's tush.

I CAN COUNT THE NUMBER of people in this world that I trust on a sawmill worker's hand. Nick is one. He knows what I won't ingest. Heroin. Angel dust. Ice. I assume he and Hoppy score every night, but they seldom show up with something I won't try. Powders are the exception, but even so, with one dab, Nick can tell me what's in any given synthetic. He just can't tell me how much.

AT THE PODIUM TONIGHT WHILE signing in, I hear Herrera calling another pit to request two more 21 dealers. Apparently, Phoenicia Timmons and Danny Wilson are no-shows.

"I need two bodies," Herrera tells the other pit boss. "Got any to spare?"

And when Dead Bob asks me, as he's been doing at the start of each shift, "So are you going to put on a suit or not?", it finally sinks in, that in this place, you're either spare change or an empty wallet.

A NEW ENTRY FOR THE PLUS COLUMN: No more crap from crew. Angry? You bet I'm am. I almost stick-whipped Number One tonight, right across his new bridgework. Not that he started it. Max did with his innocent comment about a new men's store opening up at Meadowood Mall. But Number One hunkered down like a Rottweiler and wouldn't let go.

"A suit," he said, staring at the top of my head, an old trick, just to get my goat. "A paid voyeur. A company hack. Hope you're ready for some major ass kissing. Pucker up, Buttercup. For management and players both."

"I think he has nice lips," Liz said, which only made things worse.

"He'll need them," Number One said. "Better buy some lip balm. And some knee pads. And apples and some Pledge polish. I hope your nose prefers autumn colors."

Because Max started it, I ended up going off on him instead of Number One.

"You'll look good in a suit," Max said. "If that's what you want."

"How would someone like you know what I want?" I asked him.

Afterward, I was sorry. And vexed. The P and M score is now a tie.

NICK DOESN'T WAIT FOR ME to answer the door. Any light on is an invitation to enter.

"We need you to settle a bet," he says and unwraps his palm to reveal a small, somewhat elliptical shaped pill. "Dr. Hoppy can't find it in his pharmaceutical bible. I say it's a hit of ecstasy. What do you think?"

I bring Nick's palm up to my face, resisting the urge to lick its contents. "Looks like ecstasy to me," I tell them.

"And circle gets the square," Nick says, eating the pill.

"Hey, what about the judges?"

"Sorry. This is all the guy had on him."

Says Hoppy: "We need to upgrade our clientele."

THE ONLY TIME MY FATHER CAME to Reno, he kept his watch set on Eastern Standard Time. On my day off, I suggested a drive to Lake Tahoe. At the top of Mount Rose where we stopped to view the vista, he turned to me and asked, "Is this what you wanted to see?" His yellow tie flailed in the afternoon zephyr, a caution flag. I told him that all my ties are clip-ons, that if a customer grabs me by the tie, that's all he's going to get. The good Controller who probably wears a tie to bed asked me what the customer normally got. We drove back to Reno in silence.

YOU'D THINK THEY'D KNOW BETTER than to have a new suit sit box on a high-limit game, but DeLuca and the shift manager like to put their rising stars on our game. Tonight, we had a supernova.

Tonight, this new suit decides to be the dice police, making sure every player throws them in a timely manner. It almost costs the club a player with a credit line as big as Guatemala's GNP. Wes, who Number One says owns the construction company that has built every 7-Eleven in the Bay Area, likes to take his time with the dice, shake them, talk to them, have his fleshy wife blow on them. It's all part of his routine and if these histrionics prevent an extra roll or two, then they make up for it in attracting other players who are drawn by Wes's exuberance. I don't mind Wes. He tips.

The new suit has other ideas. And after his third reprimand, he tells Wes that if he can't shoot the dice properly, then he can't shoot dice. Wes's response is to pick up the crimson cubes and drop them in his wife's Bloody Mary. "I'll do anything I want," he says and looks to his wife for approval.

It takes the casino manager ten minutes to calm Wes down. Wisely, they move the suit to a different pit. I'm on break for most of this, but I still get brought up to the pit office along with the others to file an incident report.

Liz, who takes all this to heart, says that as the stickman, she should have intervened, that it's her responsibility to pace the game.

"It's your job to educate your players," DeLuca says, not to Liz but to me.

This gets a rise out of Dead Bob. He asks DeLuca, "Is it also our job to educate our pit bosses?" He too looks at me when he speaks.

Only Max fixes on DeLuca when he says to leave Essex out of it if the crew gets written up since I was on break when the flame-out occurred.

DeLuca dismisses Max's beau geste with a smile so broad, I see two gaps where there were once teeth. I wonder if they were pulled out or knocked out.

THE KNOCK ON THE DOOR that I've been waiting for still catches me by surprise. It's Nick, alone, with something else to offer.

"We got a call," he says. "You want to come?"

I've just taken off my shoes and am two sips into a beer and would prefer that the mountain come to Muhammad tonight, none of which concerns Nick.

"Yes or no?" Nick asks. "We're not maître d's. We can't make them wait."

"I'm in," I tell him. I realize I'm still wearing my black and whites, but Nick's look tells me I don't have time to change. I locate my shoes.

The vacancy of the cabin I'm riding in surprises me. I thought I'd be surrounded by all sorts of medical equipment, but what startles me more are the attitudes of Nick, who's driving, and Hoppy. "Got a one car," Nick says. "Driver exited through the windshield."

"We may not get to stay and play," Hoppy says in the same steely tone. These are not the loadies who seem more comfortable in my house than I am.

Our drive is a short one. The siren doesn't sound for long. At the scene, Nick bypasses the policeman directing traffic, another who's setting up flares. He drives by the mangled car just beyond the curb where the driver lies. Nick and Hoppy put on plastic gloves, hand me a pair, then leap from the front seat, open the rear door, begin removing equipment. "Come on, Essex," Hoppy shouts. "Time to load and go." I exit the cabin, bump into a policeman who looks at me with concern.

"He's a trainee," Hoppy tells him. "Come on, Essex." He hands me the backboard, races ahead. I carry it like a surfboard, then a shield, desperate not to blow my cover. I want to look at the car whose engine parts lie strewn over the road like spilled intestines. I want to be mesmerized by the glimmering glass path that leads me to Hoppy and Nick. I want to take this all in, the randomness, the suddenness, before it's all explained.

"Come on, Essex," Hoppy says.

I can't see the victim's face because Hoppy and Nick are bent over him applying a c-collar, but I recognize the half-inch cuffs and penny loafers. I almost drop the backboard that Nick grabs from me. Hovering over everyone, I feel like the angel of death. I think Max senses my presence. I know I should say something, but the hideous taste in my mouth makes any word I say seem like a drop of poison that could kill him. So I watch.

"Don't worry, buddy," Hoppy is telling him. "You're in good hands." And then to Nick, "He's ABC. Vitals are good. Head and back lacerations. Possible collapsed lung. I'll check for broken ribs." And then to me, "You know this guy?"

I just nod.

Hoppy kneels beside Max, but his attention is fixed on the approaching policeman. He leans into Max, whispers, "The cops will screw you if they find drugs in your car. If you have any, tell me where they are and I'll remove them."

"Tell him, Max," I blurt out.

Max turns his head toward my voice, shrieks in pain.

"Don't move," Hoppy says. "Wink once if your car is clean."

Apparently Max does. "Come on," Hoppy tells Nick. "We've got a scoop and scoot."

I watch them load Max into the back of the ambulance as if they're doing no more than shoving a pizza into an oven. Hoppy follows him in.

Nick again turns on the siren. "I'm sorry about your friend," he says after rolling down his window and spitting.

"Payday!" Hoppy says. "I knew it!" An orange plastic vial flies into the front cabin. Nick picks it up, examines it, drops it suddenly. "Christ on a crutch," he says and lets go of the steering wheel long enough to wipe his hands on his pants legs. I pick up the vial, hopeful, and begin to unscrew the safety cap.

"I wouldn't do that," Nick says.

"Why not?"

"AZT." He looks at me. "Friend of yours, huh?"

"We're on the same crew."

"I'll bet you are," Nick says. "There's one drug I hope I never need."

I drop the vial. I wonder what kind of buzz AZT provides then realize that I'm doing it too, scrubbing my hands against my thighs. I know it's Max, but I can't stop.

I'M SITTING IN MY LIVING ROOM with the lights out so Nick and Hoppy won't drop by. I've taken two blistering showers and washed my hands with Clorox. I'm sitting in my La-Z-Boy, stuck to it in the adhesion of my own sweat. My last beer lays empty at my feet. Max's vial sits by the door sealed inside three Ziploc baggies.

Hoppy said there was no way Max was going to die. So after I get some sleep, and lunch, I'll probably go see him. If I do, I'll bring him a copy of Playgirl just for grins, find out what he wants to do with his AZT. If he's alert, I'll ask him for the name of the mall store that's having the sale. I'll act like nothing has changed.

But it bothers me that Max never told me. Not that I could do anything, but it would have been nice to know. I thought we were tighter than that. Now I feel like a mark. All along I've been granting Max dispensation from a sin he's never cared to commit. My life is venial. His sins are mortal. That's the real P and M list—which makes my decision easy.

BANK JOB

Essex and Dead Bob see my relief approaching our craps table before I do. I'm watching the cocktail show crowd spill out, wondering who would pay good money to see a singer who hasn't had a hit in a decade.

"Pit office," the new guy says as he taps my shoulder.

Once the dice stop rolling, I call the number, gather them in the crook of my stick, bring them to the center of the game. "Shooter is three to your right," I tell my replacement and clap my hands once to show Observation that the only thing I'm removing from the game is myself. "He's all yours," I tell Bob and Essex, who love to pimp any dealer new to our crew. But they're not smiling. Their pinched looks reflect their distrust of the pit office.

Which is no revelation. Sometimes you get pushed out for a performance review and maybe a raise. But a slap comes more often than a pat. More often, some pit boss wants to write you up for breaking a procedure. Or for making a significant mispayment. Or for ruffling some player's feathers. That's my guess. Last night, I reprimanded a player for pastposting bets on my blind side. This guy purposely waited until I was bent over the game paying other bets before laying down a bet and then claiming that I hadn't paid him. When

43

I told him all winning bets had been paid, he protested. Loudly. Short men always do.

I climb the thirty-six steps to the pit office wondering just who this guy complained to and how big his credit line is. I stop for a drink of water at the cooler by Wardrobe. A new thought. Maybe they're going to tell me I've finally been promoted to the floor supervisor position that was posted a month ago. They've already turned me down twice. The first time, they said I needed more experience and suggested I learn another game. I learned two: roulette and pai gow. The last time, my shift boss told me they were looking for someone more assertive, someone willing to use his spurs.

"You mean a man?" I asked.

"I mean a chief, not an Indian."

I realize now that my shifter was testing my mettle, that he wanted me to respond, to act like a chief, so he could give me the promotion, but his words numbed me. They were just another reminder that all my life, people have expected me to be someone else. Even my mom. When I was twelve, I had a chance to make confession with the archbishop of our diocese during his yearly visit to our parish. I didn't. It wasn't that I was self-conscious, which is what my mother thought. I've never been that, even about my height. It just seemed that my lying three times, swearing twice, disobeying my mother four times, and coveting Marie Disotelli's ruby ring were small-potato sins unworthy of the archbishop's forgiveness. These were anybody's sins. My sins needed to be peculiar to me and disturbing to him. Not mortal sins. Just my sins. From him, I wanted absolution for something I'd never dare do again.

My mom was crushed. I had denied her the chance to show the other parishioners that a single parent could raise a penitent child. So she offered her own absolution, exacting on me the penance of civility. Even after I got caught stealing a wallet at Woolworths, she treated me with dignity, as if my reluctance to confess meant I was incapable of sin. Eventually, I felt perhaps I *had* done something profoundly wrong. Since then, I've assumed that every act carries the potential of sin.

THE DOOR TO THE PIT OFFICE is closed. A test of my assertiveness? I suck in my breath, put on my game face. If they tell me that I've been promoted, I won't gloat. If they turn me down again, I won't stew. And if I've been summoned for a write-up because the indignant player has a high enough credit line that my bosses have taken his side, I'll accept the write-up without objection. Pat or slap, I'll wear the same face.

Seated inside this windowless room are my shift boss, the casino manager, Larry, the pit boss who runs our shift, a house security guard, and two men who identify themselves as policemen. I catch myself tugging at my waistband, a nervous habit.

"Sit down, Elizabeth," the casino manager says.

"Liz," I say. I only let my mom call me by my full name. I take the only vacant chair. No one seems anxious to speak. I'm tugging at my waistband again. The security guard smiles at this.

"Do you know why we're here?" one of the policemen asks.

"Are you speaking metaphysically?" Their looks of concern tell me I've said something stupid.

"Can you tell us what you did when you got off work last night?"

"I picked up my tips. I met a man at the bar. We went out for breakfast." The security guard is still smiling. I fold my hands in my lap. "Did I do something wrong?"

"Was that gentleman William Cremens?"

What was my tell? I'm sure I didn't flinch, but I've done something to make them shift in their chairs. "Yes." Again, some of them squirm. "What's going on?"

The other policeman unbuttons his jacket. He leans forward and speaks slowly, pausing pregnantly between each word as if it's our little secret that Billy Cremens is dead. "He jumped from the top of the Sagebrush Savings Bank parking garage four hours ago. He was pronounced—" My raised hand stops him.

"Do you want a Kleenex, Liz?" Larry asks.

I shake my head no. And I don't cry because I know that's what they expect from a woman.

"Can you tell us about your involvement with Mr. Cremens last night?" the first detective asks.

I'm not sure because now Billy does seem like some Mr. Cremens.

"You're not under suspicion," he says. "This is just for our report."

I stare at my interrogator to let him know this isn't about civic duty. I sit up, grasp my hands, stare down the security guard, and tell them—some of it.

I tell them that Billy played on our game last night, bet his usual five-fifty across, bet his usual progression, press, same bet, press, same bet, won a little, drank one or two scotches, had a good time, tipped the dealers, left. I tell them that I always have a drink after my shift, but that running into Billy was accidental, not prearranged though I wonder now if that's true.

I tell them that we had a couple of drinks, that I never have more than two drinks, at least not where I work, before we went out to the Peppermill for breakfast. I tell them, yes, we did spend the night together but at my place, not in Billy's room, that I've never spent a night in a hotel room with any man.

Larry nods approvingly.

I tell everyone that Billy left at noon today after showering, shaving with one of my razors, and fetching a change of clothes from the rental car he followed me home in.

"There's no report of a rental car," the second detective tells the first who writes this down.

They want to know: Did Mr. Cremens say or do anything that seemed irrational? Did he seem morose or suicidal? Did he talk about death? What *did* we talk about?

"The game," I say, which puzzles them. "Craps. He wanted to know if his betting system was a good one or if he was beating a dead horse." The word catches in my throat. "Is he really dead?" And if I shudder momentarily, it's because I've caught myself feeling not sorrow or horror or pity, but relief that I'm not being accused of anything. Billy Cremens is dead and I'm playing blameless.

"We're sending you home for the night," my shift boss tells me.

"No! No. I'm okay." I smile for them. I want to finish my shift.

The casino manager and my shifter look at Larry, not me, for approval. "Let her," Larry says.

"Thank you, Miss O'Donnell," the first policeman says. "We're sorry to put you through all this."

I want to ask them if Billy left a note, but I'm afraid my curiosity will be taken as an admission of implication. The five one-hundred-dollar chips I found on my bed stand have already accomplished that. I stand up, nod weakly to these men, realize I'm dusting my hands as if leaving my game. "He was only thirty-four," someone says. I make my way down the hall to the women's room, clutching the wooden railing so I won't fall. I wait until two cocktail waitresses leave their perches in front of the mirror before I choose a stall to weep in. Billy told me he was thirty.

WHEN I RETURN TO THE GAME, Dead Bob, Essex, and Max are dealing at ramming speed, trying to rid our game of its final players so a pit boss can lock up our game and send us home. Apparently, the rookie sent down from the pit office is on break. Max, sweet Max, who is due out next, taps his watch. "You're not due back for five more minutes," he says.

"You take it," I tell him and grab the stick from Essex. "There's work to be done here." That gets a rise out of Bob, no small feat. I call a number, wait for my crew to rotate and let out Max.

"Well?" Essex asks. And though Bob would never show it, instead, he just stares at me with his Mount Rushmore face, I know he's just as curious.

"Well?"

"Billy Cremens." This is too much like confession.

"What about him?"

"Dead. A bank job."

"No way!"

I nod. Still no concern from Bob.

"What's your tie-in?" Essex asks, a fair question, but before I can respond, I feel the hands of my replacement caressing my back, palming and pressing my shoulder blades as if they were my breasts. I bring the dice back to the center of the game before the shooter realizes they're no longer in front of him. I run my grip halfway up, then thrust the pole straight back so that it catches the hard-on behind me squarely in the stomach. I tell him that no one puts his hands on me, ever, unless I want him to. I look at him, making sure he understands.

"Miss Congeniality," Essex tells the players on his side of the game. "She's a welcome wagon with legs."

I return the dice to the shooter who's now afraid to pick them up.

I CRIED THIS MORNING. I can't believe I'm still doing that. I thought being assigned to the 4C craps crew, getting to deal with Max and Essex and Bob, who the other dealers call the Legends, would free me from attachments.

It's not something I like to admit, it broke my mother's Catholic heart, but like a lot of other women, I too rode the trail of tears to Reno to establish my six-week residency so I could divorce. It's not failing at marriage that bothers me. Or failing my mother. Or the church. It's knowing that I am no different than all the other women who tossed their wedding rings into the Truckee River, then stayed and found work in a casino because it was the best thing life could offer. I hate the notion of following this migratory path.

At first, I told myself that I wasn't like the others. I was educated. I had an M.A. in English from Berkeley. I was a community college instructor, in line for the next tenure track position at Foothills. I wasn't pinned down with children. I was in control. I was the one dictating the terms.

But that wasn't true at all. I realized this in a courtroom full of strangers the morning my divorce was granted, and later, when I found myself drifting through the casinos, seemingly with the same clump of people. As if I (we) were nothing more than a swarm of gnats newly hatched in the dead summer heat. Alive. Adrift. Aimless.

I meandered for a week, in no hurry to return to California, to the condo I'd leased. Why not stay? It was summer. I had no courses to prepare, no papers to grade. I stayed in a different hotel every night. I slept without an alarm clock. For seven days straight, I drank more than I should, gambled more money than I'd brought, bought tee shirts I knew I'd never wear. I stole a wallet from Macy's just to see if I could do it right this time. I kept it for a day, then returned it after substituting a picture of me for the one of the model. I began paging myself over casino PAs just to hear the sound of my name. Liz O'Donnell. It was the only time anyone said my name. At the end of each day, I sat on my latest bed staring at the phone, willing someone to call, but no one did. At the last hotel, when even sleep grew tiresome, I found a keno lounge large enough to hide in and stayed awake for fifty hours—until I understood that the world was much more vast and imposing than I'd dreamed, if I'd ever dreamed at all. Forever, I'd wanted to be my own person, but the sad truth was: I was as anonymous as my latest hotel room and no more distinct.

On a whim, I responded to an ad in the *Gazette-Journal* and was accepted into a dealing school at the Aces Oasis. I learned to deal 21, what the Legends, even I now, call skirt work. It quickly became as tedious as the women I worked with who sucked down diet colas on their breaks and waved their cigarettes like highlighter pens while showing snapshots of their children or their pets when they weren't busy discussing a recent purchase or who was now doing their hair. I talked myself into the next craps school by convincing my interviewers that I was tall enough to get to all of the bets, that dealing craps was no more physically taxing than dealing 21, that it would be good PR to have more women craps dealers. In truth, I think the casino manager liked the image of me bending over the table.

I learned my craft well. And I avoided the rivalries of the men, preferring, like a jogger, to run the course, not the race. My only concession to gender was to keep a rubber ball around the apartment that I relentlessly squeezed to strengthen my hands until I could hold as many chips as a guy.

I was ranked second in our school and immediately assigned craps shifts, but even so, I took my time infiltrating this male domain. I didn't talk on the game when I wasn't calling dice. I let it pass when someone told me I was pretty good—*for a girl*. Instead, I watched and picked up moves from other dealers. I learned to drop-cut chips, how to snatch and grab and when to convert a player's bankroll to a higher color. I didn't wear a wedding band like some women did to keep the creeps at bay. I met their advances with indifference. I never used my gender to cut a corner. I never used sweetness to assuage an angry player. And I refused to wag my tail for a tip even on nights my crewmates competed to see who could hustle the most tips. I remained innocuous, like the white-on-white shirts I wore. I refused to play this game on the game.

I've never understood this competition thing men have. It's a coal that burns inside them, a gray lump that's instantly set aglow by the slightest wind of provocation. I think competition is a weakness because it requires someone else. Maybe that's my reason for leaving my marriage, teaching, the church. I've never wanted to be better than anyone else. I've just wanted to be good. To matter.

The powers-that-be thought I was good enough to be scheduled on 4C which didn't sit well with the Legends. I was replacing Number One, Michael Davitz, who had been banished to some low-limit perimeter game for telling, or rather, for getting caught telling a female player to go take a flying leap against a doorknob. A lesser dealer would have been fired.

Dead Bob resented me the most. He called me Number Seventy-Three. Even when there was heavier action on Max's side, he watched my end hoping to catch a mispayment. I bore his distrust. I didn't return the favor when it was my turn on the stick. Instead, I waited him out. For a month. Until I caught Bob napping on a buy bet.

"You got another bet to pay, Bob," I said as softly as I could.

"That's Mr. Bob to you," he said, dry as dust.

"If this takes any longer, that player's bet will be as deceased as you."

Essex broke up. So did the pit boss lurking over our game. So did Bob. I'd fanned their coals. "Pay the man, *Mister* Deceased Robert," Essex said. Bob looked at me with one of those *I've seen everything but the wind, done everything but die* smirks of his. He too had been waiting.

IT'S A GOOD THING I DON'T WEAR much make-up because I've been crying on every break. The cow eyes I get from Essex, Max, and even Bob make it worse. They look at me like I'm Billy Cremens's widow. Each break, I tell myself this time will be different, but as soon as Max taps me on the shoulder, I dust my hands, make my way to a casino restroom, hide inside a stall, and empty my eyes.

If they have their coals, then I have my ice cube. As much as I'd like to be sweet, to be overwhelmed by everyone's kindness, appreciative of my crewmates' concern, even fancy that maybe Billy and I had started something, believing, hoping, that I can still feel the crush of love—I can't. The truth is, I'm not saddened by Billy's death; I'm angry. And that scares me.

I'm certain that Billy was waiting for me at the bar two nights ago. I don't normally hobnob with players. I get enough of them on the game. And the last thing I want is to look like some skirt worker anxious to find a sugar daddy who can offer her a way out of this town. But Billy Cremens is, was, a genuinely nice guy, and I'm not saying that just because he tipped the dealers. I saw him once ignore a dealer's mistake that cost him a three-hundred-dollar payoff just to avoid getting the dealer, new and nervous to high-limit action, in trouble. Billy didn't act like a player. He never flashed his money. And he didn't walk around with his fly open like so many men. On the game, I was just a dealer to him, just another Legend, though sometimes it felt like what he said in that kind and patient voice was directed at me. Certainly, some of his looks had been. So I sat down beside him that night and told him that sitting by himself at this time of night was a dangerous thing to do.

"I always pay my way," he said. "But I've never paid for a woman. At least not with money." Which led us to admit the things we *had* used as legal tender. Liquor. Lasagna. Flowers. Mending. A set of tires. Pride. In that hour, Billy never turned away from me, even when reaching for his drink. His eyes were crayons, coloring me in. I agreed to have breakfast with him if he'd tell me why he was still drumming the bar rail after I'd asked him twice to stop.

"I'm stuck inside this flesh prison," he said. "I'd give anything to be someone else." I asked him what he meant. "I'm
stuck," he repeated. And again, "Stuck," as if he needed convincing. I left to fetch my sweater and collect the night's tips,
unsure if he would still be at the bar, but there he was, staring
watchfully at the escalator. As soon as he saw me, he raced to
help me with my sweater. We left full drinks. We walked arm
in arm along the sparkled sidewalk outside the Cal-Neva.
We took the elevator to the top of the Sagebrush garage
where Billy asked me if I wanted to share a joint with him.

Then he did the thing that won me over. Or did me in.
When I said no, he put it away. He said he wanted to remain
on my wavelength.

I opened up like a clam. Against the cement wall overlooking Center Street, I told him everything. Why I don't
wear skirts. Or carry a purse. Or believe in Mr. Right. How
nuns and mothers can make you feel guilty about sins you
haven't committed. What I would give to have thick, curly
hair like his. How glad I was to get to know him away from
the game.

"So who would it be?"

"Who what?" A bad ploy, I thought, his wanting to com-
pete with some man I've never imagined.

"If you knew you were going to die, who would you want at
your deathbed? What's the very last thing you'd like to see?"

"Probably a slice of cheesecake."

He avoided my glibness, turning his gaze to the street
below.

"Maybe the faces of all the people I've loved. Or better
yet, all the people in the world who've loved me, though I
couldn't tell you who that would be."

"I'll bet you'd fill a stadium."

"Maybe a confessional," I said. We stood there in a puddle of silence and I thought: every room is a confessional. "What about you?" I wanted to ask him about being stuck.

"I don't know." I caught him drumming his ringless fingers on his legs; I grabbed his hands. "Certainly nothing that reminds me of myself. I'm not sure I'd want anyone there. Death doesn't seem like something worth sharing."

We had breakfast in a corner booth on the Virginia Street side. "You order for me," he said when our waitress finally found us. "I'm so tired of my own taste."

Billy ate slowly, more interested in my stories about community college politics than his omelet. Over breakfast, I told him more about me than all of Reno knows. I tried drawing Billy in. I asked him twice to explain why he felt stuck, but both times, he sloughed it off. "It doesn't matter," he said.

"Everything matters," I said. "Or should." I was talking about myself.

I paid the tab. I grabbed the bill folder from Billy's hand, gave a credit card to our waitress, listened to him protest about always paying his way. Over his shoulder, the desert sun was rising, casting off light against his silhouette. He looked like one of my mother's holy cards of the saints that she keeps on her bureau. As we stood, I noticed a twenty he'd slid underneath his plate for a tip. St. Billy, patron saint of heavy tippers. I stuffed the twenty down his shirt which made him laugh for the first time. I felt contagious. I thought: this could work.

And because he never asked, I did. At my place, I let him undress me, then I undressed him which he seemed to like more. It was hard to tell. He kept his eyes closed the entire time. It seemed like he was wincing.

MAX, NOT ME, IS THE ONE with the new boyfriend. But as graveyard pushes out our crew, he makes a point of nodding toward the bar.

"Do you know who that was?" he asks after moving anything emblemized with the corporate logo to another table. Tonight, I told a marker player that when I wanted crap out of him, I'd squeeze his head. "That man owns TechnoComp."

I sip my Kamikaze. It tastes good. Maybe I'll have three of these tonight. Or four.

"You're blowing it, Liz."

"I was the last person Billy Cremens was intimate with."

"You don't know that."

"Oh great. That makes me feel a lot better."

Max's fingers play trumpet around his highball glass. I've embarrassed him. "He picked you. He made the choice and it was you."

"Hey, I had a say in this too."

"Exactly." Max orders another drink for me.

"I was at his last supper. I *was* his last supper."

"Don't get religious on me," Max says.

"He took his last shower in my bathroom, got dressed for the last time in my apartment. Maybe I was the last person he spoke to."

"Don't."

"I was the last person he slept with."

Max gathers my hands with his, hands that are softer, shapelier, better manicured than mine. He puckers his lower lip, forces me to smile. "You mustn't blame yourself," he says. "No one could be that bad a lay."

IN MY BEDROOM, IT'S DARK AND COOL. I sit on fresh sheets while the Washoe zephyrs blow through my screens, flaring my beige curtains like pennants. The wind keeps extinguishing my candle. I've given up trying to keep it lit.

They buried William Cremens today here in Reno, not in San Jose, which the newspaper reported as his hometown. The obituary notice listed no surviving family members or relatives. It failed to mention who made the arrangements.

I didn't go. It would have felt like I was playing widow. It's enough to wear my black and whites to work, to see all the looks of pity, even from craps dealers who barely know me. Apparently, word has gotten out. No one speaks. They're all waiting for me to respond, to grieve, but I won't give anyone that satisfaction.

I didn't go because I was afraid to see who did. I was afraid that maybe there would be a wife and family there although Billy didn't wear a band. Maybe a mother anxious for someone to blame. Or worse, no one. My curiosity seemed a shabby reason to attend.

I didn't send flowers or have a Mass said. I didn't pause to reflect at the hour of his interment. I didn't do anything because as much as I hate to admit it, I'm still angry.

I'm angry that Billy chose a bank job. Didn't he know the media would trivialize his death? SAGEBRUSH SAVINGS GARAGE CLAIMS ITS FOURTH VICTIM. I feel like the Catholic Church, which considers suicide a mortal sin. I'm condemning a dead man which doesn't seem fair. That should be the sweetest thing death brings, release from expectation. But I'm furious with Billy because he played me. All the time I was telling him about my life, he was staring past me looking for a way to end his.

Later, in the bed I now sit on, I caught him doing it again. Holding me but looking past me, eyes open, as if he wanted me to be someone else. As if he wanted to be somewhere else. I grabbed him by the hair. "You look at me," I told him. "I'm your vision. You look at me." For a while, he did.

MY CREW STILL TREATS ME like I'm Mrs. Cremens. Tonight, when I told this slowpoke player that I was trying to read his mind but that he wasn't giving me much to go on, it was Dead Bob who stopped the game, calmed the player, and explained the correct procedure for announcing bets. He didn't give me his bemused look.

Their manners are insufferable. Essex, who's chronically late, now returns promptly, resolute that I get my full break. Max makes it a point not to overrun me even when a pit boss tells him to speed things up each time our game starts dumping. Even the relief dealers who work our days off watch my end of the game. They don't want me to get written up for making a bad payoff. Everyone pities me. No one trusts me.

Our crew has always prided itself on its bad attitude. After all, we are the Legends. But lately, I seem to be the only source of rudeness. Fine by me. I'm no merry widow and I let the players know it.

"Shooting or rooting?" I ask the timid wives who stand behind their husbands.

"Only farmers get rich in the field," I announce whenever a tourist wins a field bet.

"There are no secrets on a craps game," I tell anybody who'll listen.

I HAVEN'T SLEPT WELL SINCE Billy died. I changed the sheets and threw out everything I thought might still carry his aroma, or his aura. I even buried the five chips in the ficus planter, started my own little graveyard, but it didn't help. Since the night I dreamed that his side of the bed *Listen to me! One night and it's his forever* had turned into this sinkhole with a gravitational pull I couldn't escape, I've tried sleeping elsewhere. On the floor, then on the living room couch, then in the hammock out on the porch. Nothing works.

Yesterday, I visited his grave which surprised me. I would have thought someone like Billy would have chosen to be cremated. I thought there might be an inscription on his gravestone, but there was just a name and dates. I couldn't bring myself to kneel and pray; it would just be another confession. Why confess if there's no chance of absolution?

I walked around the cemetery startled by the number of piles of freshly dug earth. These graves—were they already consigned?—looked like big marmot holes, and I wondered if there ran from grave to grave an underground network of tunnels. There was one section overlooking the junkyard on Fourth Street that was a family plot. On a slope above the Truckee River, generations of Yardleys have been laid to rest in what seemed to be a horizontal family tree. No fresh dirt piles here. Three of the deceased Yardley women shared the same name. A mourner would have to check the inscribed dates to know which Felicia Yardley she was praying to. Only the women's graves had flowers, plastic ones, adorning them. I removed a bunch from the oldest Felicia and laid it in Billy's holder. Then another bunch, then all the Yardleys' flowers until Billy's grave was completely covered. I combed the cemetery for more flowers, just the plastic ones, and laid them crosswise over Billy's grave. I wanted to give him wings.

A plane passed overhead. I jumped up and down, waving frantically. Nobody noticed. Perhaps the plastic flowers didn't reflect well. I looked at the grave and couldn't decide whether I'd made a cross or an x. I rearranged the flowers to spell BILLY. I waited an hour for another plane. None came. The afternoon shadows made me drowsy so I lay down beside his grave. I put my ear to the ground, waited for him to tell me why it was me he chose, what made me better than the rest. If I come here again, I'll bring my own flowers. Real ones.

I'M DOWNTOWN, WALKING AMONG the tourists in the searing heat, trying to tire myself to sleep. It's been over a hundred for a week straight, but that's not the cause of my insomnia. I'm eating a hamburger from the Nevada Club, dripping grease as I make my way down Douglas Alley toward the square on Center Street that they've turned into a bus pavilion. I've dripped grease down the front of my blouse, but it doesn't matter. I sit down on a bench, toss the wrapper and remaining bun into a receptacle, catch myself staring at four teenage boys, two in red, two in blue, who are playing a raw-edged game of stare-down.

Their eyes light on me like bees before returning to their own concerns. Any second, I think, I could witness gunfire. Perhaps be shot. But now I'm staring, hoping to catch their attention, wanting an answer to Billy's question. You, wearing the turned-around Kansas City Royals baseball cap, what would be the last thing you'd want to see if right now one of the ones in red, someone as young and as angry as you, emptied his pistol into your body? Would you want your final vision to be blue? Would the blue waft of smoke from his gun suffice? The blue sky about to grow forever black? Or would you make some desperate attempt to see a face? The girl you've gotten pregnant? Your forgiving mother?

You, tourist, clutching your plastic bag stuffed with tee shirts. What's your final vision of joy? Three bars all lined up? A slot machine spewing coins? Bus driver. A run of green lights? That rider you've never spoken to?

And you, little girl with the cast on your leg, tell me. Is it nothing more than a scene from your favorite television show? Can you conjure any image at all that's your own or does death wear someone else's face? Tell me that you see more than the ugly pair of shoes your parents bought for you and made you wear. Tell me that it's not your ex-best friend who wrote the dirty word on your cast. Or the word itself. Tell me that the choice of what we finally see is ours. Our doing. And tell me why Billy left a message on my answering machine to let me know about the chips. Explain to me what way he has paid. Tell me how he found my coal.

THIS TIME, SOME DEALER tells me specifically whom I'm supposed to see in the pit office. I pay the last of my place bets, clear my hands, and thank the only player who's made bets for us dealers. "Thank you, sir!" I say loudly. "You're setting a fine example for the other players." Essex and Max flash me different shades of misgiving.

I take my time getting to the pit office. I chat for a minute with a bartender who has begun running in marathons. I show my watch to a woman who wants to know the time. By the stairway, I look out at the sea of tourists seated in long galley rows, each one paired with a slot machine. Above all the din, I hear one woman celebrating a jackpot. She has my mother's timbre.

There's only three of them waiting for me this time. No policemen. No security guard. Just Larry. And Ernie the Pencil, the swing shift schedule maker, who looks peeved. And my shift boss who tells me I'm being given a week on the street. He says that no one here, not even a Legend, is indispensable. He suggests I use this time to think about my customer relations and what sort of image I need to project on the game.

"A week on the street," I say. "Well, that's longer than Billy Cremens got."

No one laughs. Instead, they stare at a manila folder bearing my name that my shifter thumbs through until he comes to an empty page. So I'll understand the gravity of the situation, he has waited to write in my presence this latest entry. It's my first black mark, the first time the casino has found fault with who I am.

I take my time reading and signing it and afterward, I linger. I'm tempted to ask someone to fetch me a drink of water or maybe a cup of coffee. I want them to feel as uncomfortable as I do. But no one fidgets. Or speaks. I'm the one who finally yields when Larry frowns at me to show his disappointment.

In the hall, I stop for a drink of water, holding back my hair while I drink deeply before continuing on to Wardrobe where I wait for a woman bent over the engraving machine to sense my presence. When she does, I hand her my red plastic coat check.

I notice a line of blank name tags and a roster sheet by the engraving machine. "How many of those things do you make in a day?" I ask.

"Ten, maybe twenty," she says. "You people drop them like seeds."

"I'll bet you've made hundreds of name tags."

The woman likes my curiosity. She stops looking for my jacket. She throws her hands on her hips and smiles. "Thousands, honey. I even make them in my dreams."

"Would you make me one?"

"Did you lose yours?"

"Yes."

"What's your name?"

"Billy. But I'd like Mrs. C."

"I can't, honey," she says. "No Mr. or Mrs."

"Make it Billy."

"That's an odd name for a girl. Is that with a y or an i-e?"

"You decide," I say. "I'm so tired of my own taste."

When she hands me the name tag and then my jacket, I leave her all the change in my pocket, five silver dollars.

"Thank you, honey. You have a good night." She scurries away, anxious to return to her machine.

Downstairs, I order a drink at the bar, a throw of the dice from our game. I want to gesture to Max what's happened. And show the Legends my name tag. Then I think better of it. Anyone of them, even Essex, will see through me.

I take my drink with me. I cross the casino air curtain and head for Second Street. Where I'm waiting for the light to change is probably no more than fifty feet away from where Billy landed. When the walk sign flashes, I step out into the crosswalk into the path of a Cadillac that wants to get curbside.

I jump back, spilling my drink, cover my face with my free hand, breathless, feeling that the car has already run through me. A wave of nausea brings me to my knees, face flush with the pavement.

So tell me, Billy. What was the last thing you saw? Was it something tucked away in your psyche like some shirt in your closet you forgot was there? Was it your signature on a contract you had no intention of fulfilling? The thing that made you feel stuck? Or was it just the gray macadam of Center Street, the anticipation of pain, your bones about to shard and tear? Was it the enormity of your mistake? Something you meant to tell me? Was it your choice? Was it me?

TRUE ODDS

9/2

Tonight, James will park his sports car by the railroad tracks then cross the parking lot, careful to avoid stepping on broken glass. Inside the Aces Oasis, he'll check his jacket with wardrobe, stash his keys and wallet in a locker, run a comb through his hair. At five minutes to six, he'll push into 4-C along with his crewmates, spelling the day shift crew, and begin dealing craps on a high-limit table. For eight hours, he'll take, pay, and place bets. He'll call the dice when it's his turn and afterward, offer to fetch his crewmates' tips while they wait for him at the bar.

He'll expect to get razzed if the small envelope he hands each of them contains less than a hundred dollars. He'll listen to his crew recount the night's game, the weird bets players made, the pit boss who wouldn't stop sweating the money, the size of the woman's diamond, the flea who wouldn't leave the game. He'll buy a round whenever it's his turn. And when the conversation turns as it always does to his mail-order bride, his Garden State babe, James will tell them the painful truth.

By then, he'll know what degree of remorse to show. He won't feign indifference. He won't deny a thing, and if Max and Essex and Dead Bob press it, he'll admit it, that he was dumped, a shocker, like Tyson falling to Holyfield.

Surely, his bluntness will make them uncomfortable. They will cease calling him Just Born Jimmy, his latest nickname. For a change, they'll peel away first. But James won't leave just yet. He'll take it all in, the 21 dealers in their still-perfect hair, the newer craps dealers anxious to talk shop with a high-limit dealer like him, the pit bosses holding court in their own circle, the late-night players, drunk, chasing their lost twenties with hundred dollar bills. He'll politely refuse someone's offer to go in on a gram of blow. He'll avoid getting too friendly with some 21 dealer who assumes he's lingering intentionally. He'll drink each bottle of beer slowly.

And when he senses from his windowless perch the initial slashes of sunlight, James will go cash Phyllis's final check, the one he found wedged in his doorway with his name misspelled, and do something stupid with it like gamble. By this time, he'll have been awake for forty hours. But he'll put off for as long as he can going home to a bed he hasn't slept in for weeks.

8/31

THEY STAY UP ALL NIGHT, HER SUGGESTION, playing 21 and sipping champagne from plastic glasses. James loses steadily, his luck like gravity, but he feels obliged to keep playing even though she finds his losing streak amusing.

"Here's to Reno, the biggest little suction cup in the world," she toasts in her New Jersey accent each time he loses a big hand. "And to legionnaires" and makes him bump his glass into hers. "And to Legionnaires' disease" and tries to spill his champagne.

At ten minutes to nine, they cash in Phyllis's winnings. James reminds her to tip the dealer. She tells the bartender to keep their champagne on ice, that they'll be right back. He tells her that the bartender is not pouring from their exclusive bottle, but she doesn't believe him.

They walk to the courthouse, shielding their eyes from the sun. Phyllis hands him a Certs and takes one for himself. "Back in a flash," she says when they cross the Truckee River.

Hers is the fourth case on the docket, the third divorce proceeding. In each case, the judge asks the female plaintiff if the recorded grounds, irreconcilable differences, is correct *Yes* and whether there is any chance of resolving the conflict *No*. Then it's the residency witness's turn.

James takes the stand determined not to let the judge see that he's drunk, but when the judge stares at him like the divorce is his fault, James finds it impossible to stare back. Instead, he looks at Phyllis and is stunned by a look from her he's never seen. Gratitude. When asked, he tells the judge *Yes* he has seen Phyllis Turnbull every day for the past six weeks at the same Nevada residence. When excused, he takes his place beside her still unable to return the judge's look, to convince him that he has a legitimate stake in all this.

Afterward, he waits outside while Phyllis takes care of the fees and paperwork. He arches his back and feels his muscles pop. For once, she has been the one wanting to extend the night, but that's not why James isn't in the partying mood. There is a loss here, James knows, a sadness that sunlight and slot machines and ninety-nine cent breakfasts and new love and a signed document can't recoup. He wants to ask a lawyer carrying the leather valise what makes a good witness. He wants to go home, to *his* home, and sleep. He wonders what excuses he can offer when she suggests that they continue the celebration.

He sees her on the other side of the thick glass doors and instinctively stands. He holds out his arms, waits for her to walk into his hug, but as soon as she hits the courthouse steps, Phyllis is off and running and doesn't stop until she reaches the Truckee River bridge. There he finds her tossing her wedding ring up and down like an apple. "This is the best day of my life," she tells him.

He stares at the rocks in the shallow river. "Things couldn't have been that bad."

"They weren't," she says. "I just didn't like being married. I never knew where I stood. Now I do." And before he can stop her, she flings her ring upstream into the thickest part of the current. "Due process," she says and is off again running.

James is too tired to chase her. He assumes that she'll be at the Aces Oasis sipping champagne, waiting with a glass for him, but she isn't there. Or in any of the downtown casinos. Or at the motel where he has the cab driver wait while the desk clerk tells him that Mrs. Turnbull checked out yesterday.

8/30

HE PUSHES PAST THE HAWAIIAN shirts and the pastel polos he keeps on hangers, selecting instead a black knit shirt. He never used to wear black or white on his days off. The last thing James has ever wanted to be is colorless. Or locked into just one look. As he's told other dealers at parties, the desert needs all the splash it can get. But Phyllis told him that he was a handsome man, that color on him was a distraction. She's gotten him to buy blacks and grays and deep purples, death's colors, he tells her each time they go shopping. And while James prefers that dressing be instinctive—he never lays out clothes on his bed ahead of time—tonight, at her request, he will wear all black. He doesn't mind. This is her night.

He's grateful that she called but wonders why the change of heart, especially after today's tirade. Her stubbornness has become an attraction. At her apartment this afternoon, as she lay beside him crushing cigarette butts into the telephone mouthpiece, *I hate telephones; only cowards use them,* she said that she wanted to be alone tonight, that she'd meet him tomorrow on the courthouse steps. When she said nothing more, James got dressed, left. He obliged her by not offering to pick her up beforehand. Was she having second thoughts? But four hours later, while he was wondering how to spend this extra night off that he'd wrangled a month ago from the schedule maker, she had called, capitulated, asked him to meet her downtown at the club where he worked. He insisted on another casino where the dealers wouldn't know him.

He doesn't question her change of heart; he's surprised by it. It's her first vacillation in the forty-eight days he's known her. Normally, he doesn't like people who keep their lives perpetually tidy, but the broom handle seems to fit her strong, stubby fingers. He's learned that her choice of shoes is not a casual decision, that she smokes Marlboros because they're not a new brand, that his refusal to use an alarm clock bothers her. It's no surprise that she disputes his claim that Nevada has its own time zone. NST. He learned early that she's more comfortable indoors, surrounded by walls.

Not James, especially not inside a casino on his night off. That was the second time Phyllis got peeved, on her second day in town when she assumed his refusal to take her to the clubs to play 21 was a reflection on her. It was, in part, but he had passed it off, explaining that he couldn't bring himself to make someone else do something he himself hated doing.

Inside the Money Mountain Casino, he wonders why he agreed so readily to tonight's rendezvous. And why Phyllis is so curious about craps. Twice, she stops at an empty game and asks him to explain bets. He's happy that she's finally taking an interest in what he does. He wants to ask her where they stand, where the divorce tomorrow will put him. Instead, he corrects her, *It's true odds, not at odds*, and explains what true odds means. He says it's the only bet the house pays according to actual occurrence, knowing that Phyllis doesn't understand. He tells her that every other bet is a loser, that even when you win you lose because the house is taking a cut of your action. He talks about parlays, not about the two of them. He doesn't want to seem pushy, not after her tantrum this morning when he got slapped for asking her to move in with him.

"Great," she said. "And maybe you could put a homing device on me or just chain me to the bed when you're not home."

"I thought it would save you money," he said. He wasn't about to explain the foolishness of paying for two beds when they were only using one.

"Money? Is that all I am to you?"

"Phyllis," he said as calmly as he could, the word sounding false.

"You men," she said. "Eddie was the same way. We didn't have a marriage; we had a merger."

He told her that he didn't speak for all men, that he was just one man.

"You're not even that," she said and slapped him again.

So instead of finding out about them, James tells her that hard ways are pairs, that proposition bets are sucker bets despite their high payoffs. He tells her that only farmers get rich in the field, but she doesn't get the old joke. He asks her if she'll move in with him if he buys her a craps table.

"Not a chance," she says.

8/11

HE WON'T BE LYING TO THE JUDGE about her residency. He goes to her motel room every night now, at three in the morning after shift, earlier on his days off. He endures his crewmates' chiding at the bar when he begs off after the second beer. They call him American Gigolo. Spencer for Hire. Pussy whipped. Just Born Jimmy and wave their pinkies at him. Do they sense his urgency?

It's not because Phyllis doesn't have a car that he goes to her place. He's offered her the use of his Miata, something he thought he'd never offer anyone, but she won't accept gratis from him. "I'm not a leech," she says each time he offers.

He goes to her place because she won't go to his. She claims she's allergic to his cactus. He thought she'd be impressed with the layout, with his sense of color. "Why would anyone own a plant that doesn't have leaves?" was all she asked.

The second time he brought her to his place, she aimed her disbelief at him. "What am I supposed to do? Stay up and wait for you at your place hoping you'll come home soon? No thanks. I've already done that." She demanded to be driven back immediately. "A kept woman," she kept repeating during the ride until it felt like he was running over speed bumps.

He thinks that Phyllis is afraid of gratitude. He thinks that she regards any luxury as tax, unlike the casino women. So her room with its sweaty linoleum floor cracked in all four corners, the loud air conditioner she insists remain running all night, the cinder block walls, the floral plastic curtains, the vinyl and chrome furniture, the one overhead light, its austerity as constant as the shadows it casts, no longer bothers him.

Nor does her smoking. Or her harsh East Coast accent. Or her too-blonde hair that fools no one. Or her make-up that never comes off. Or her skinny thighs. Or the resolution in everything she says and does. Or her thing about putting everything in its place. He thinks the room could use a little clutter, but lately, she's taken to sweeping the floor with a newspaper. Or the fact that she's thirty-five, a decade older than him, the reason his crewmates now call him Just Born Jimmy.

"How can you be sure she's not your mother?" Essex asked him one night at the bar. She isn't the woman James pictured falling in love with, but like he told Dead Bob and the others, "It's not the worst thing that ever happened to me."

And it's not. He's unsure that she understands when he tells her what it was like to be an only child, what it felt like the first time he shot a deer, his fear of trains, how he wants to get a business degree at UNR, then an MBA, that dealing isn't a forever job for him like it is for Max and Essex and Dead Bob. He's not sure she cares to grasp any of it. And if he's reluctant to tell her that he loves her, it still feels good to tell her things, these reminders of himself.

It also feels good that they talk when doing what she calls afterward *performance*. He doesn't mind that she doesn't always mask her disappointment. Or that much of what she says sounds like instructions. It feels good not having to feign control. The only time it doesn't feel good is when she starts railing about men. All men, not just the one he is replacing.

In the morning when her alarm goes off at 10:10, James redresses in his black and whites because she doesn't want a set of his clothes around the place. She won't say why. He watches her put on one of three bathing suits. He walks with her alongside the fence that hides the sunbathers from the ceaseless Virginia Street traffic to the motel pool that reeks of chlorine. She detests the display, but he always kisses her before leaving.

At home, he immediately showers, checks his mail, pays bills, takes in or brings back his laundered white shirts, places bets for the two of them at the sports book, deposits his tips into his checking account, has lunch. His time with her has made him realize how little maintenance his life requires. And how its greatest offering is its immediacy. Purposely, he never enters the sports book prepared. He assumes there will be written in chalk on the big, sliding boards names of starting pitchers that will attract him. Darling. Swift. Smiley. If there are no names that beg to be bet, he bets on team names. He bets on A's to beat Jays since they precede them in the alphabet. He assumes Pirates will beat Padres, Indians will slaughter Rangers. Rock, paper, scissors. It's how he regards himself and Phyllis.

8/6

AT THE BAR, WHEN MAX WAS CERTAIN the others were out of earshot, he told James he could still summon the smell of his ex-wife's breath.

Phyllis stays in James's mind only when he hears her speak or can touch her. At night, her clenched, closed eyes remind him that he's forgotten again to ask her if it wouldn't be better if she moved in with him. When she rolls away from him, he inches over to the sag on his side. He lies on his back and listens to the din of the air conditioner. It amuses him to think that maybe she smokes so much because she's from New Jersey and is used to breathing used air. That maybe chlorination, not Clairol, has made her hair that way. He tries to imagine other places they could be.

When he's dealing craps, he never thinks of her at all.

This past semester, a marketing professor at UNR told James's class that everything precious already exists. Air exists, gold exists, land, oil, diamonds, wood, water. The professor said success was simply a matter of discovering what is already there. "Create a demand," the professor said. "Control the supply. That's why gold is expensive and limestone isn't. It's why a good painting, or even a bad one, costs more to own than the best-written novel."

Each night, when James lies on his half of the bed, he tries to think of things no one else has ever done before. It bothers him that nothing he has done surprises her.

"Can't you manufacture worth?" one student asked the professor.

"Certainly. What real purpose do diamonds serve? How much better is a Lexus than an Acura? Closer to home, think of the genius who decided to call apartments condominiums so he could sell space instead of renting it. Or the fashion designer who saw the wisdom in sewing labels on the outside of her clothes instead of the inside."

James has to control his shivers. It's not the air conditioner. He stills himself, not wanting to awaken her. He wants to do something noteworthy, but his professor's contention that most creations are calculated acts, not spontaneous ones, disturbs him. So he tries to imagine other places they could be because it's easier than envisioning her. He can recall what Phyllis looks like in a bathing suit, but when she is sleeping beside him, turned away, he has no idea what the look on her face might be.

7/24

"COULDN'T THEY HAVE BUILT this road any straighter?" Phyllis asked on their ascent up the Mount Rose Highway.

"I have money for you," James said. "You won your first baseball bet last night."

"How long is this going to take?"

"Did you hear what I said?"

"I don't want your money. I'm getting a divorce. I'm not filing for orphancy."

At the crest above Lake Tahoe, he tried again. "It's your money. Both Martinezes won. A double Martinez. Your drink. Your bet."

"This road sucks out loud," she said.

For the first time, he took an extended look at her. Her toenails were one shade of red, her fingernails another, her lips a third. Her hair was a shade of blonde he'd only seen on dolls. He guessed she wasn't a swimmer. Or by the looks of her pasta-colored skin, a sunbather. Sand Harbor was out. She probably just wanted to be driven around. When they came to the T in Incline Village, he turned right, away from the beaches, toward the casinos in Stateline before he bothered asking her if she swam.

"I do, but I'm not swimming in this lake," she said. "I don't swim where there's fish."

She didn't respond when he asked her kiddingly if she wanted to go to a nude beach, so he drove on to Tahoe City past the bridge where the Truckee River began. He drove to the Sunnyside where they ordered lunch and watched tourists dock their rented sailboats. He thought her black jeans and matching long-sleeved shirt that hid her tube top marked them as tourists too. Like two tagged pieces of luggage.

"Wouldn't you love to spend a week on a sailboat?" he asked. "Sail to Emerald Bay. Sail down to the casinos. Eat at a different restaurant every night. Most of the lakeside places have docks."

"I like these drinks."

"We could live like pirates. Do you sail? I could teach you how."

"What is it with guys?" she said. "Why isn't a regular life enough? Eddie was the same way. He always wanted to be somewhere else. Doing something different."

James asked for their check. He watched Phyllis adjust her top.

"It's all crap," she said. "All you guys want to be captain just so you can push someone around. Let's get out of here."

He let her walk away. If she wanted to think that leaving was her idea, fine. She wasn't going anywhere without him. He turned his gaze the other way, toward three panicky tourists who were approaching the dock at a dangerous angle. Even if she was giving him a blast he didn't deserve, the day was too good to throw away. He watched the three give slack to the wrong sails as their eighteen-footer eased into a slot between two other boats. A perfect docking. At the car, he suggested again that they go for a swim. "It'll cool you down. We can buy some beer. I'll pour one in the lake. That'll keep the fish away."

"I want to go back to the pool."

At the confluence of Lake Tahoe and the Truckee River, they watched a group of vacationers bent over the bridge, watching the jumping fish. James steered away from the way they had come, took Route 89 instead, past the glut of river rafters below, the Squaw Valley turn off, the town of Truckee, onto the interstate, past the border where he saw a sign that said: NEVADA—RECREATION UNLIMITED. They spoke only once, on the mountainous stretch outside Hermiston where he told her to quit throwing her matches and cigarette butts out the window. He said that people out west didn't do that.

She asked why it mattered. Said there was nothing here to burn.

He said the world wasn't one big ashtray.

She lit two cigarettes and tried to hand him one.

At the motel, she almost burst into tears. He followed her in and they laid down together behind drawn curtains. For a while, he listened to her recount her husband's betrayals. He imagined himself, them, on a sailboat on the lake at night, drifting. He pictured their anchorless craft bobbing in placid water, forming perfect rings. He remembered Max saying once that a person had just thirteen minutes to get out of Lake Tahoe once he fell in. James stopped listening to her mischances. He felt only the lift of the waves, saw sails of black and red.

7/23

IT WAS NOW PART OF JAMES'S ROUTINE to get to the sports book by eleven, before the start of the East Coast afternoon games. He knew little about baseball. He had no idea who was in first place or who played in what league. Instead, he bet like he did at the racetrack: on names he liked. He always bet on the team that owned Armstrong, the perfect name for a pitcher. Today, he wired up Armstrong with a pitcher named Gooden, another name he liked. On a whim, he bet a parlay for Phyllis on two pitchers named Martinez because that was what she drank. He'd never met anyone before who actually drank martinis. It seemed like such an adult drink. From a different era like highballs or old fashioneds. It made him aware of their age difference.

James dreaded the final thirty yards to the Aces Oasis sports book, an aisle that ran between two long rows of 21 tables. He avoided the eyes of the day shift dealers, pretended not to hear their *hellos*.

It wasn't like this two years ago when, as a rookie fresh out of craps school, James was all eyes, unnerved by the ubiquitous beauty of the women dealers, each one a stunner. The girls he knew in Oregon didn't look like this. Even more astounding was their self-assurance. They were the ones who started conversations, bought drinks, patted behinds, referred to people as lays. Initially, James was put off when each night, while the swing shift dealers waited at the bar for the night's tips to be collected and parceled, one of them would openly hit on him. That it wasn't his idea made him uncomfortable.

Then it dawned on him that he was living a drunkard's dream and wouldn't always have access to such women. So he let his wife for the night buy him a drink, take him by the arm, lead him to her house. Angela, who wanted to show him her new Range Rover. Becky, who was dying to show him her horses. Stacey, who told him they could spend the night at any one of the three houses she owned.

This string of one-nighters ended when one of them failed to recognize him in street clothes at Park Lane Mall. Even after James reminded her of their week-old tryst, he sensed that she either didn't or didn't want to remember his name. At that moment, he understood that he was just currency. Immediately, he removed himself from the after-work bar scene which didn't sit well with several 21 dealers who had come to rely on his availability.

"What are you, a snob?" one of them asked him in front of her friends. "You?"

For the next month, James waited in the cafeteria after work until tips were ready. He stopped seeing swing shift dealers. Instead, he came to work early and approached a few day shift dealers he'd eyed. But their schedules, their kids, their willingness that hung on them like price tags, never made for a fit. He retreated to the circles of men at the bar at the far end of the casino, resigned to talk shop with other craps dealers and pit bosses. Until Phyllis, it had been a year.

Outside the sports book, he checked his bets to make sure they were right. Martinez and Martinez, a two-team parlay, thirteen to five odds for twenty-five dollars. He avoided the wave of one dealer but was forced to answer when another woman twice called out his name. He nodded stiffly, embarrassed that she'd caught him looking at her name tag. He snapped his fingers as if he'd just remembered something, retreated to the sports book. He decided to double up on Phyllis's bet. Lately, he'd begun feeling guilty about being a man.

7/17

ANYONE KNOCKING ON HIS DOOR at this time of day couldn't be someone he knew. James hastily put on a pair of cut-off sweatpants and opened the door.

"Phyllis Turnbull," a woman said behind gauzy cigarette smoke. "Tom's friend. Actually, his sister's friend. I just met Tom a month ago when I decided to do this."

He invited her in, watched the trail of smoke follow her, wondered if all people from New Jersey brought their pollution with them.

On her own, she found a seat in the living room, one of the leather Strat-o-Loungers by the television. He knew she was looking for an ashtray and in a minute he'd bring her one. But right now, he wanted to size up this thing who seemed unconcerned that her red lipstick clashed with her purple eye shadow, who'd dyed her hair an impossible shade of blonde, who wore all black, even her go-go boots. Typical East Coaster, he thought. Everyone wants to be the bad guy.

"Here's half," she said and threw a check at him. "Let's get this done right away." She let her ash fall on the carpet. James brought her a saucer. "Is it always this hot?"

"Yes." He watched her fold gum into her mouth. He hoped she wasn't planning on staying with him the entire six weeks it would take to establish her Nevada residency. Who knows what Tommy might have told her.

"You live by yourself?"

He nodded. What gave it away?

"That's the best way," she said, and now James felt secure enough to ask her where she was staying.

He'd never heard of the place. It wasn't downtown. Probably one of those places on South Virginia or Fourth Street a person could rent by the month. He'd find out over lunch.

When he returned from his bedroom in a tee shirt and slacks and his lizardskin Justins, he found her hanging up the phone. He assumed she had made a long-distance call.

"Don't doll up on my account," she said.

"I thought we'd have some lunch," he said. "I could give you a tour of the town. Get you some fresh gum."

She tossed her cigarette into the kitchen sink. They both heard it sizzle. "Don't do that," he said.

She stuck her gum on the wall beside his phone. "I don't care if you like me or not," she said. "I don't need your cowboy crap."

"I'm going downtown to gamble," she said. "What else is there to do in Helltown?"

"What time tomorrow?" she said and closed the door.

6/22

I'VE GOT A PROPOSITION FOR YOU, Tyrone Tommy had said over the telephone, one that could turn into a business. Said she was willing to pay James five hundred bucks just for telling the judge he'd seen her every day. Said that she was a friend of his sister's, a flake, that it would be a good idea to ask for the money upfront. Tommy said it was a bad year for relationships. Said there would be others to follow.

PHOTO OP

The first time Jerry tells me they want to see me upstairs, I think he's kidding. First off, there is no upstairs, except for the nine hundred guest rooms. Second, we're Observation. Nobody ever sees us. At least they're not supposed to.

But when Jerry nods toward the door, I understand what this is about. "Watch Third Base on 4-21," I tell Al who's on the big surveillance board, the one we call God. "I think he's counting down her deck." I grab my wallet—I don't like carrying a purse, it draws attention—and make my way to the metal door.

Behind me, I can hear Al muttering something that causes Jerry to snicker. If Al gave the scam artists on the casino floor below us the scrutiny he gives me each time I enter or exit, this casino would be crime-free. He always waits until I'm out of earshot before mumbling something to someone else. I've done nothing to encourage him. I've even taken to wearing baggy pants and sweaters, but that hasn't deterred him. Or Jerry. He's started doing it, too, those darting looks that never quite become eye contact.

But their corked lust isn't why I'm being summoned. This is about my request to have my picture printed in the upcoming issue of *Your Aces*, our employee magazine. Last month on page 6, they ran the name and picture of each department's rep to the Board of Review, the Aces Oasis grievance board. If you have an issue to resolve, you can take it to the Board where a guy from management, another from HR, and someone from your department supposedly decide your fate. It's really just a dodge to keep out the unions. The vote is always two to one.

In the last issue, they ran everyone's picture but mine. They printed my name but left a blank square above it as if I were Harvey the Rabbit. Or somebody's guardian angel. Twenty-four names but only twenty-three pictures. It's not right. Even Jerry, who wouldn't flinch at the Second Coming, said it was their loss. Since I'm the department rep, I couldn't take it to the Board, so I spoke to Bob Bennett, my shift boss, who now sits before me beside a woman with plucked eyebrows and silk-wrap nails who identifies herself as Heather Langley from Personnel before she asks me what I want.

"I want what everyone else got," I tell her. "Recognition. I want my picture run and an apology for the omission. This isn't just for me; it's for all of us peeks. You tell us how important we are to the casino, but you treat us as if we don't exist." I'm really talking to Bennett. "It's not right."

"We're Observation," Bennett says, as if I don't know that. "We *don't* exist."

The irony here is that I remain silent.

"How's this?" Ms. Personnel says, her sympathy as genuine as her hair color. "You give us a picture that's not indicative of your present appearance and we'll run it in the next edition. Fair?"

I feel like one of those obituary photos taken thirty years before the person died. Bennett agrees to her stipulation before I do.

"We go to print in ten days," she says. "Act fast."

THE NEXT FIVE DAYS ARE AS BAD as my first week when a player I fingered as a pastposter turned out to be the casino manager's tax attorney. Apparently, Bennett has leaked it out that I want exposure for all of us peeks. Everyone acts like I'm wearing a wire. Al, who usually lets me take lunch last, I get too sleepy otherwise, now pulls rank and takes the last break. Jerry now buys his own smokes instead of bumming mine. Even Ted, who's new, treats me like I'm radioactive. I've got a reputation for being able to capture on camera any scam move, but not once this week has anyone asked me to shoot video. They spend even more time now scanning the casino for a "photo opportunity," their code for cleavage. But now, they're self-conscious about it. About me.

I could store all this, wait for the day when one of them needs me to swing a bat for him at a Board, but I let it pass. I'm trying to decide what to do for a picture.

My first thought was to go to the mall and have one of those glamour shots done. I'm no traffic stopper, but I'm not unattractive either. Since I don't wear make-up, I thought a glamour photo would cast me in a different light. I thought it would cast a favorable light on our department as well. Eat your hearts out, craps dealers. You too, bartenders. And you, Al. You want something to leer at? Here you go. You too, Jerry.

But when I got cold feet and ran the idea past Jerry, it was like he was standing in a campfire. He hopped back and forth, clearly uncomfortable not just with the idea of my wanting to push people's buttons, but with the fact that I didn't see anything wrong with doing this. When I pressed him, he said, "You have no idea who's out there or what they could do." Then he moved away. From me, Ms. Uranium.

After that, I thought about really dolling myself up, wearing that off-the-shoulder number I've always been too chicken to wear, just to let Jerry and everyone know how little they do know about me. But I knew *Your Aces* wanted just a head shot. What then? A baby picture? My decade-old prom picture? I thought about a photo of the back of my head but realized that for many of the floor workers, my back was as familiar as my front. I thought about a mugshot, one of those grim side profiles, but knew that would never fly past Personnel. Or me. I wanted the picture to reflect our department, but I also wanted it to say something about me.

THE PICTURE I CHOSE I TOOK MYSELF. Had it developed at One-Hour Photo and barely got it in on time. To my surprise, they ran it. There was no apology for the omission, just a brief explanation and my name and picture above it.

I knew response from Bennett was destined. What I didn't anticipate was Al and Jerry and Ted now looking me in the eye when they spoke, which was mostly to ask what possessed me to comb my shoulder-length hair forward so that it cascaded down my face. Or what I used to section it in strands to make it appear like I was looking through prison bars.

I didn't care to explain it to them. I was savoring my meeting with Bennett, planning how to express without seeming boastful the vindication I felt I'd won for us peeks.

My amusement was short-lived. My expectations of what? Amazement? Chagrin? Respect? were quickly replaced with my own dismay when Bennett spoke of the irrefutable damage I'd done to the department. He pointed his finger so close to my face I could have bitten it when he said I would never go any higher in Observation, not as long as he was running the show.

HUNCHED OVER GOD, AL AND JERRY were eager to hear what happened. They turned away from a possible dabber on 12-21 and looked at me wide-eyed, impervious to my shame which hung on me like bird dirt. True peeks. They had no concern for me. They wanted only to eavesdrop on my conversation with Bennett. I told them nothing.

Then it happened. After lunch, last break was once again mine, a gift bestowed on me by Al in hopes of coaxing a confession, I saw a woman in a stained, frayed dress pastpost twenty dollars on the first blackjack she'd been dealt in an hour. Her move was clumsy, no pro here, and I was surprised that the dealer didn't notice. The woman had been making just five dollar bets. Such a bump, especially on a snapper, should have been a giveaway. Procedure calls for running a camera on a cheat, document everything for the arrest, so I began shooting film. Three hands later, she did it again on a pat twenty which beat the dealer's eighteen. I shut off the camera, reached for the phone, then watched, stunned, as this woman tipped the dealer one of her ill-gotten nickel chips.

I put down the phone. I erased the tape without notice, not an easy thing to do with Al and Jerry around. And for the first time, I watched.

What I saw was this woman, still cheating yes, but still tipping, her generosity more primal than her honesty. I saw middle-aged couples struggling to have a good time, knowing they should in a place like this, but not knowing how. I saw an old man, grumpy with the knowledge of having nowhere else to go, berate the play of every tourist who sat beside him. I saw an Asian woman hand her last chip to her grateful husband to bet and lose. They were slow to leave the table. He finished his cigarette while she reassembled the contents of her clutch purse. Even after he helped her with

her coat, they lingered, smiling, arm in arm, their bad luck
a constancy they could share.

I NEVER WENT TO BED THAT NIGHT. I waited until Personnel
opened then waited outside her door until Ms. Heather
Langley realized I would wait her out.

She brought me inside her pastel cubicle, pointed to where
I should sit, waited for me to initiate conversation.

"What do you want?" she finally asked.

"A new job."

For my sake, she went through the motions of studying
her computer screen for job openings before studying me
at length. "How does cocktail waitress sound?"

I smiled.

"They make good money."

I shook my head, mostly at the thought of becoming a
photo op.

"What then?"

The question caught us both by surprise, made us look
openly at each other. What I saw before me was a twenty-
five-year-old woman yearning to be perfect. Professional.
The other thing I saw was myself merely observing, peeking
through the eyes of God at a person not impatient with me
but with herself. So I told her this: "I want *your* job."

HERE'S THE JOB SHE OFFERED. I'm in Personnel on the
ground floor. I love saying that, considering my former position. I'm the low person on the totem pole although the
first person I said this to corrected me, said that the most
important tribe member was always placed on the bottom,
not the top. In my new position, I file, write letters, and
sometimes interview to fill the minimum-wage positions

when the main reps like Heather are buried. But mostly, I take the file pictures of all new hires.

I don't take the DMV type pictures my predecessor took that all share this numbing sameness. Each picture I take must reveal something about the subject. So I take a moment before snapping the shutter. I talk to each new hire. I find out where they're from and where they want to go. I think each one of us is a totem pole, so I try to capture as many of their faces as I can. The new custodian who was once a dancer at Arthur Murray's. The new cocktail hostess still unsure of her beauty. The new peek staring blankly at anything but me.

DEAD BOB'S STORY

Across the table from me and Number One and Just Born Jimmy, this new craps dealer offers a hundred dollars to anyone who'll paint a mustache on the portrait of our CEO, Edwin Church, that hangs ten feet away on the cafeteria wall. Says it's a standing offer. Says it loud enough to make the table of 21 dealers in the booth beside ours look up from some baby pictures and giggle. I don't help Number One and Jimmy and this rookie with their scheme. What interests me more is the heft of the cafeteria silverware, especially the spoons, heavier than any socket wrench I own. And the new plates, shinier than hubcaps. And the electric bug zappers that have been mounted like speakers in the corners of this room. It's been a fierce winter, hardly bug weather. But except for when the power flickers off, which is happening a lot tonight because of the wind, the zappers stay lit. What a waste.

That's the part that gets me. If this casino is doing so well, then why are they trying to push me out the door? Sure, I'm one of the few dealers who makes top salary, but it's only forty-four dollars a shift. What's the big deal?

It is a big deal to Raynelle, who's using all her juice to find out why it's me who gets to walk the plank this year.

Every January, when business dies, they weed out a few of us veterans and a few rookies, usually the flashy types, just to let everyone know how shaky their jobs are.

The guys at my table have decided that the Edwin Church caper could only be pulled off on a slow night on graveyard. I scope our section of the cafeteria, seeing if I can pick out anyone else who might be under the gun. My eyes catch on JB who immediately stands up as if he knows what I'm thinking. As if it's my decision whether he gets canned.

As soon as JB rises, all of us swing shift dealers do. It's twenty after; our break time is over. We return our dirty utensils and dishes to the bus stand then file down the hallway like cattle, past the hotel elevators to the escalators where, at the bottom, we head to whatever pit we're dealing in. Me and Number One and a half-dozen 21 dealers, all of them real lookers, return to Pit 4 where the high-limit games are. This casino learned a long time ago that if you're going to lose your money, it might as well be to someone you can stand to look at. They've always had the nicest looking women here at the Aces Oasis.

And for twenty-two years, I've enjoyed looking at them. It bothered Raynelle at first, catching me looking, but hey, I got married, I didn't go blind. And the truth be told, I think Raynelle was flattered that she was considered attractive enough to deal in Pit 4 although she hasn't dealt there in a while. She thinks that's why they want me out. She thinks it's because I've lost some of my hair, and what's left has started graying. She wants me to grow a mustache, says I'd be more handsome. But it's not my appearance. Or my performance. I'm the same dealer I was a decade ago. You'd think a company would reward fidelity, but they don't. The reason they want me out is plain and simple. Somebody doesn't like me.

At our craps game, Liz tells me which player is shooting the dice, thanks the players who've made bets for us dealers, clears her hands, then hands me the stick. I send the dice out to a bent little cowboy who immediately rolls a seven that kills the hand. He glares at me before gathering his chips and leaving. Several other players look at me with disgust, as if I'm dripping with AIDS. Some leave. Some don't.

"Curse of the new stickman," Max, who I think *is* gay, tells the remaining players. I wait for my crew to push through and let Essex out on a break before sending out the dice to the next shooter, a woman who apparently thinks craps is played like roulette. She drops chips everywhere except the one place she needs to.

"Drop one of those chips on the pass line," I tell her. She sets a twenty-five-dollar chip on the pass line as if she's laying down a mousetrap.

"Kind of like shopping, isn't it?" I tell her. The overhead lights flicker, go dark, then just as quickly come back on. The woman stares at me, upset, as if the power shortage is her fault.

I call the number after the dice she's thrown finally come to a rest. I urge her not to throw the dice so hard. I tell her that craps is a game of skill, not a game of strength. At the podium inside our pit, all three pit bosses have gathered. I'm no egomaniac but I swear they're talking about me. The youngest one, always the worst, is staring at me, daring me to do something rash. I smile at him and return the dice to the shooter.

My guess is that they're figuring out another way to get me written up. Twice this month, I've been pushed off the game, sent up to the pit office, informed of my latest sin, asked to sign this newest work history entry, warned to straighten up and fly right, then told to return to my game where my crewmates look at me with concern—or with relief that I wasn't fired.

Which may or may not happen the next time. Normally, it's three strikes and you're out, but with my time in, they may give me an extra at bat.

That's how they nail you here. They build a case against you, document everything in writing, and make you initial each entry to show that everything has been above board. When there's enough entries, they wave your work history in front of you like it's a big surprise. They've already got me down for not picking up a losing bet, which is pure crap, and for totaling payoffs, a procedure violation that is common practice anywhere else. I almost smiled when I read that one. I was surprised the observation boys had figured out what I was doing.

"Seven out, line away," I call, ending the woman's hand. More dirty looks from the players. Two more pick up their chips and leave. I don't send out new dice to the next shooter. Instead, I watch the young pit boss approach our game. He walks like he's trying to avoid wrinkling his suit. Ten feet away, he gestures for me to drop the stick, but I wait until he says it.

"Go wash your hands," he says. "They're disgusting."

And for a moment, damn him, I feel shame. Not because of the grease that lines my knuckles and fingernails, but because of the attention he's drawn to me. Everyone, even Liz, now stares at my hands. A young couple leaves.

I stare, expressionless I hope, at this young smoothie who can't even grow a full mustache. I don't say a word, which is what he wants, lip, the final straw that will give him just cause to fire me. I clap my hands once and leave the table. I won't give this punk the pleasure of firing Dead Bob.

That's what they call me, even some of the new dealers who don't know me. Among the craps dealers, it's important to have a nickname. Jim Burns isn't Jim; he's Just Born Jimmy because of the way he feigns surprise whenever a customer points out the obvious. Michael Davitz, who's been here longer than I have, is Number One. Frank Meyer is Oscar. Pam Pershing is Spray Pam, and before that, Madame Tussaud. There's Essex, the Jaybird, Uncle Remus, Radar. The dealers here are as bad as the tourists. They're all caught up in the casino neon where everything has to be more than it is. They don't understand the worth of a primer coat. They notice only the waxed and buffed enamel. So they make everyone someone else.

Even Raynelle. She asked me once on one of those days when I knew she was angry with me for paying more attention to a Volkswagen than to her if I'd ever cheated on her, or if I ever wanted to. The way she asked made it seem like she almost wished I had, that my doing something unlikely, even something sneaky, was attractive. I swear that's why she wants me to grow a mustache. So that I'll look like someone else. I stayed underneath the rear axle until she went back into the house. I've learned that some questions don't have a right answer.

So has the casino.

Essex gave me my nickname the night this woman with possibly the best set of knockers God ever made, certainly they were among the biggest, fell out of her dress while bending forward to pick up dice I'd purposely left short. Even Max went bug-eyed. When I didn't, Essex said, "Doesn't anything get a rise out of you?" When I shrugged, he said, "You're dead, Bob, I swear it. You died in your sleep and don't know it." From then on, I became Dead Bob.

Maybe it's true. Maybe I am dead. But it's better being this way than to be sucking up to people for tips which a lot of dealers do. And it's a yard better than stroking the schedule maker or the pit manager, which I think Liz literally did, just to get put on a good crew, get good shifts, or certain days off. I won't stroke anybody. Like the bettor on Thanksgiving who thought he could get me to smile by betting for me.

"This is Bob's bet," he announced each time he threw in a hundred chip for himself and a twenty-five-dollar chip for me to bet on eleven. "Me and Bob are partners."

I did thank him when I finally called an eleven. "Four hundred and down for the dealers; thank you, sir." But this wasn't enough for him.

"How about that, partner?" he kept repeating and wouldn't roll the dice I'd set in front of him. "How about that, partner?"

My response, as Essex tells it, was to gaze at the player's foot-long bankroll of chips while telling him that real partners split everything fifty-fifty.

I'm lying, of course. Working here is one big eight-hour stroke. If I had real money—and in a year or two Raynelle and I will, finally, have enough for me to open a VW repair shop with lifts, computer diagnostic machines, everything—I sure wouldn't spend it in a casino forcing people to wait on me. These people don't want happiness; they want recognition. That's something I can't give them.

And I'm not dead all the time. If you want to talk, come see me during the day when I'm out in my driveway working on someone's Bug or Ghia. I'll talk your ear off. Ask Raynelle, who made me get my own private phone in our garage because I was tying up our house line talking to the local parts stores.

That's the first shift I pull, the job I really want, and if I don't recognize you at the casino, it's because I don't recognize myself. Not when I'm wearing black and whites and polished shoes and a dealer's apron, pushing around people's bets, inhaling their greed. Not when I'm making gestures that aren't natural but are now routine, like calling men I don't respect "Sir," or having to keep my nails short, or clearing my hands whenever I touch cash to show observation I'm not stealing house money. I've done that at the supermarket, dusted my hands after handing the cashier a twenty. But the worst of it is that the pit department's witch hunt has made me distrustful. Even of Raynelle. On a night when we both had the same breaks, I saw her laughing at something her pit boss said, but it felt like she wasn't laughing at what he said. For a moment I wondered, until I realized I've become suspicious of everyone I don't know.

Like now. I'm about to enter a men's room on the casino floor, a procedure violation, employees must use employee bathrooms, when something tells me to look around. Sure enough, an observation goon is tailing me.

Him I will recognize. I smile, wag my finger at him so he knows, then make my way up the escalator.

This whole thing has Raynelle in a tizzy. She hasn't been sleeping well and seems to mind that I have. Every day I tell her to take a nap. Instead, she goes for a drive in whatever car I've just finished working on. Sometimes, she barely gets back in time to get ready for work.

Is observation still on me? I turn back, weed through the trail of employees, looking for anyone who avoids my eyes.

No one does. Screw 'em. I'll take my time cleaning my hands. I'll also have a slice of cherry pie before I return to the game.

Poor Raynelle. Last night in bed, she actually said it might be better if I got a dealing job somewhere else. Raynelle, who sweats every paycheck like it's the last one they're ever going to print, suggesting that I quit.

I could. Working twenty-two years at the Aces Oasis won't give me anything more than twenty-one years has. But I told her what I've been telling her for the last five years: I'll work until we've got enough to open my own shop. Not one day longer. Or one day less.

Raynelle said maybe we'd been doing this too long, that maybe it was time to do something else. She doesn't know how close we are. I asked her what else we could do, but she wouldn't tell me.

Still, and this I didn't tell her, she's right. Dealing dice or cards is a young person's job. After she finally fell asleep, she always makes me form a spoon beside her, says it's the only way she can fall asleep. I propped myself against the head-board and thought about it. And the truth is, I never dreamed for a second I'd be working this job this long. We just drove to Reno for the night to get away from the valley heat.

The thought stuck with me this morning while I was dropping a rebuilt 1600 into a '71 Super Beetle Johnny Angel found in Hermiston, the idea that the age we are is never the age we want to be. When we're younger, we always want to be older so we can play Little League ball, take dance lessons, stay up later and watch more TV, date, drive, vote, get served in a bar. And then at some point, we lap ourselves in the race to grow old. It must come at night when we're asleep, or the first morning we wake up stiff, the first time we're called sir or ma'am, the first time we catch ourselves thinking we could, or worse, would have done something if only we were younger.

The last time I did something was nine years ago when I spent a weekend with this young gal I met while picking up a VW van in Modesto.

I'M STANDING IN FRONT OF A MIRROR that's bigger than the picture window in our living room. With my pocketknife, I'm removing the grease that's wedged underneath my fingernails. I'm beside this new dealer who relentlessly combs his hair that wasn't out of place to begin with. I'm so bored I'm rolling all of the grease into a tiny ball the size of a lug nut that I wrap inside a paper towel. Like it's a rare coin worth saving. Maybe the casino is right. Maybe the young ones who still regard dealing as glamorous, the ones who haven't yet lapped themselves, should be the only ones allowed to deal.

The dealer next to me wins the race between my nails and his hair. He nods to my reflection, then leaves, greeting two more dealers on his way out. They too draw up to the mirror and remove their combs.

"I'm thinking about marrying her," one of them says.

"Are you on glue?"

"I'm serious."

"Don't be," the other one says and looks at me as if I'm living proof.

"I want kids. She does, too."

"So steal some." And just as quickly, they're gone.

I take my ball of grease with me to the cafeteria. Raynelle and I can't have kids. We tried. I even took a sperm test a decade ago. Came in a cup. Asked the nurse if I was supposed to fill it up. Apparently I did. They made it sound like I'd given them battery acid.

The news took the wind out of Raynelle's sails. She grew silent for a month. She stopped complaining about the new 21 dealers, about her hair, even about me spending so much time with my cars. It got lonely. When I went down to Modesto, it was for the van. But I also went to get away. And though I didn't plan on hooking up with that gal, I didn't turn it down either. It's not the first time I've been approached. Even a few of Raynelle's friends have hit on me. It's always there for the taking in this town. But I wouldn't ever want to wave it in Raynelle's face.

When I came back three days later, it was like she knew. And even worse, accepted it. She stopped grumbling once and for all about my fixing VWs but for a different reason than before. And she never asked again whenever I returned from somewhere how my trip went or how much did I pay for the Volkswagen I'd brought home this time. Instead, we slid into this new, silent agreement. Our dream. A repair shop where I'll run the shop and she'll run the books.

She says she wants to keep her dealing job for a while after we open, until we get things going, that the money is too good not to. I think Raynelle likes being around the younger dealers.

NOT MY NIGHT. THEY'RE OUT of cherry pie in the cafeteria. The apple pie looks too gluey, so I order a lemon Danish and ask the server to heat it up in the microwave.

"You want ice cream on that?" she asks.

"On a Danish?"

She shrugs, unwilling to apologize for her boredom. I turn from her and look out at the fifty or so people talking, eating, reading, staring back in our direction. I grab my dessert and leave her a quarter tip, something I don't usually do.

We're all sitting with our own kind, dealers with dealers, bartenders with bartenders, porters with maids. I'm tempted to sit with these two nice young women from slots. Instead, I find a spot with Number One and two other dealers at the table underneath Edwin Church's portrait.

They're talking about cheating and want to know if I've ever gone out on Raynelle. I shrug like the food server.

"How do they always find out?" one of them asks.

"Pleasure is the hardest emotion to hide," Number One says. "Ask Dead Bob."

They look at me as if they've just stuck a quarter in me and are expecting a play. I eat my Danish.

"It's the eyes," the other one says. "Mouths lie. Eyes can't."

For a good thirty seconds, the ceiling lights flicker. "That's God winking at you," the other one says. Some dealer two tables down stands up. In our section, a look of urgency now crosses everyone's face.

"Seriously, you ever cheat on Raynelle?"

It's Number One who wants an answer. The other two dealers just want out. I put down my fork, stand, let them pass. The grease ball wad in my pocket feels like a hard-on. To hell with the pit boss. I'm not going back until I'm done eating.

"Have you?"

I won't answer.

"You're dead, Bob. You're six feet down."

I wait until Number One is out of earshot before I let the words roll out of my mouth like cigarette smoke. "Not in this town." And this I know: it's the reminding, not the act itself. That's the real double-cross. In Modesto, I didn't cheat on Raynelle. I cheated on myself. I did something

I'd never thought I'd do. I told that gal what I thought she wanted to hear. I stroked her.

This time the overhead lights go out for good. It's pitch-dark. I reach in my pocket for the pen flashlight that's attached to my key ring and find the grease ball. It commands. It gets me to stand, forces my hand to rise and swipe and keep swiping across where I think Edwin Church's upper lip might be.

I'm halfway to the tray return before the lights flicker back on and all the bug zappers crackle. It's not a smart move, but I look back at the portrait to see how close I came.

I've missed but not by much. Half of Edwin Church's lip and all of his right cheek sports a mustache my pit boss wishes he could grow.

MY CREW IS OUT OF ROTATION. I push out Liz on the inside of the game. She clears her hands, circles the pit, and resumes her place as the stickman.

Again the lights flicker. With a yank of the stick, Liz brings the dice back to the center of the game. We're taught to do that. Game security.

"Did you catch the blackout?" Liz asks me when the lights return to full power.

"We were out for thirty seconds," Essex says. "Total darkness. One woman screamed. I think Max goosed her."

From a 21 table that borders our game, a pit boss leans over and says to Liz, "What time's the next roll?"

Liz reddens, returns the dice to the shooter who's on my side of the table. He picks them up, glares at Liz, then sends them tumbling down the layout. "Eight, please, sweet Jesus," he says and snaps his fingers, but it's a seven Liz calls which kills the hand.

"Thanks a lot," he says to Liz.

I clear the layout of all losing bets before paying off my don't player's three winners. It's his turn to shoot and he studies the six dice Liz has set before him as if they can tell him something. Then he bets a stack of five dollar chips on the don't pass line.

"You're shooting on the don't?" the previous shooter says.

"It's a free country," the don't player says.

"But you're betting against yourself. What are you, some kind of spook?"

"Fellas," I say.

"It ain't right. This spook is screwing things up."

"Who are you?" the don't player asks. "Miss Manners?"

"Fellas," I remind them, "It's only a game."

"Only a game?" the first player says, daring me to respond. But I'm looking across the pit at Number One who's looking back at me from his empty game. He still wants to know. I nod to him. "Yes," I say out loud and it feels so good, I laugh. "Yes! Yes!"

The angry player grabs his chips and leaves. My tears of laughter feel too good to wipe dry. I'm laughing still, even after Liz's look of dismay tells me the player has gone to a pit boss to complain.

Max returns and we rotate. At the podium, the pit bosses have gathered like carrion on a carcass. The young one blocks my entry. "Pit office, Robert," he says, the words giving him pleasure.

I pass by my game. I'm still laughing until I see the looks of alarm on Essex and Liz and Max. Then, even Number One's tears of joy can't bring mine back. I don't get it. I thought this is what everyone wanted. Me, Dead Bob, alive.

IT'S BEEN A STRANGE NIGHT. I've been on break more often than I've been on the game. What they want me for upstairs I have no idea. Maybe it's the customer complaint, though I don't see how they could have pushed through the paperwork that fast. Maybe it's about my dirty hands. Or that I took my time cleaning them. Maybe it's about Edwin Church. Maybe I was wrong. Maybe this isn't a game.

But I have to laugh because I can still feel the wad of paper in my pocket that contains what's left of the grease ball. Maybe I'll paint a mustache on whoever drops the axe on me upstairs.

At the base of the stairs by a row of slot machines, I let a file of graveyard cocktail waitresses pass by. Beauty on parade. I bow to each one as she passes by, but not one of them notices. "Hello, Midge," I say to the one who serves our pit, but she doesn't, or won't, acknowledge me. Right behind her is Raynelle's pit boss. He, too, treats me like I'm invisible. "Hey, Fred," I call after him, and this he does acknowledge—momentarily. He looks at me like a kid caught with his hand in the cookie jar. He smiles weakly, waves the papers in his hand as an excuse, moves on. I sink my thumbnail into the tiny grease ball, which is now no bigger than a bullet. I think about beaning him with it. Or cramming it into the coin slot of a slot machine. Instead, I let it fall onto the casino carpet. I step aside and wait for someone to step on it, then someone else, until the grease spot becomes part of the pattern.

I'm climbing the steps two at a time. If they want to fire me, fine. I was looking for a job when I found this one. Raynelle will understand.

MARKER PLAY

The first thing Jane saw when she awoke was a tomcat marking her sliding glass doors. Quickly, she dispelled him with a thrown pillow then ran for a washcloth and spray cleaner. For several minutes, she worked hard to remove all traces, becoming angrier with each stroke. What bothered her more than the baseness of the act was the thought of being enclosed.

Jane returned the cleaner to her bathroom and threw away the washcloth even though it was part of a matching set. She washed her hands in painfully hot water before wrapping herself inside her silver and blue kimono. Upstairs, she began setting things in motion: coffee beans into the gristmill and coffee maker, a bagel into the toaster oven, herself into her Walkman—each appliance purchased with her employee discount. And each one now a vexation. The coffee maker, whose autopause had never worked, splattered coffee onto the counter when Jane tried pouring herself a cup halfway through the brewing. The toaster rendered a bagel that was doughy on one side, charred on the other. And the Walkman was playing songs Jane didn't want to hear.

She found nothing of interest in the newspaper. Even Burton's two-page spread could not erase the memory of that nervy tomcat. That the cat was male, Jane was certain. Turf was a male mindset. And now *she* was encircled. Jane set down her mug. She removed her Walkman, tossed it onto a chair that was part of a dinette set she had bought during last year's Spring into Summer Sale, noticed the indentation in the rug where a missing caster was supposed to be. She searched for the ball, then stopped, dumbstruck. She scanned the living room. The matching denim sofa and love seat, the smoked glass coffee table, the stereo unit, the teak bookshelves—each piece stood where Jane had first placed it. The caster was the only thing not in its proper place. Jane laughed at this discovery. She had marked her own turf.

No. Not her own. Burton's. Jane felt breathless. She loosened her kimono, her skin now tight and clutching. She began moving around the furniture pieces she could lift, but there was no new place for anything to go. She reshuffled her CD collection until they were no longer in alphabetical order. Until she noticed that most of them still bore a Burton's price sticker.

Jane decided it was time to blur her borders. At least the ones with Burton's on them. She would quit her job. Today.

Who to break the news to was obvious: her boss, Alan Cheswick, Floor Manager at Burton's Department Store. How was also a certainty. She would quit on the spot just to make things difficult. And to avoid any final parting shot he might fire. Jane was the last of the old guard, the only woman in cosmetics Cheswick hadn't personally hired.

When was the stickler. Quitting on arrival wouldn't work. Although Cheswick demanded punctuality from his department, he was habitually late. Besides, she wanted more people to witness her defiance than just the skeletal opening staff. But quitting at shift's end seemed equally pointless. Why work the whole shift? Jane thought about simply not return-ing after lunch. This would provide intrigue, but it would also prevent her from witnessing Cheswick's displeasure. Even worse, it might cause him to worry about her. Compassion was the last thing Jane wanted.

In the spare bedroom that served as her walk-in closet, she exchanged the rayon suit she'd laid out last night for a form-fitting electric pink seersucker dress she had never worn. Such a landmark day deserved noticeable clothes. Jane ran an iron, which didn't mist but spat, across a sleeve. Maybe she'd quit at the first customer protest, the first time someone grimaced at the scent she was offering. Maybe she'd just hand her atomizer to Pam, the new stock girl, who made no secret of her desire for Jane's floor job. Maybe she'd spray I QUIT on one of the big showcase mirrors that were Burton's trademark. Or a peace sign. Maybe she would feign intoxication from the fumes, put on a real show. The delicious indecision!

"I'M A FRAGRANCE MODEL," she'd told her mother, Alice, the last time she'd called from Connecticut. "I'm not a clothes model. I'm a fragrance model. I apply scents." And said, "I like what I do," when her mother reminded her of her per-fectly good degree in public relations. And repeated it when Alice mentioned the article in the Hartford Courant that lauded PR as a burgeoning field for women. It irritated Jane that her mother had always regarded college as little more than an obedience school that would train her daughter to respond to the proper commands. "What's wrong with a co-ed school?" Alice had wanted to know.

Her mother's homophobic suspicions made Mills even more attractive, but Jane had her own reasons for liking the college. An all-women school provided a safe haven from the outside world. From expectation. At Mills, Jane was allowed to decide her own proximity to people, to forge her own decisions, even if they were reactions, not actions. Her mother was furious when she found out that Jane's reason for switching her major from British Lit to Communications was not a career choice but one of class schedule convenience. Jane told Alice there were some things she could do on her own.

Like get married to Joseph, her high school sweetheart, who was also waiting for Jane to come to her senses. And divorced five years later, which brought her to Nevada. Over the loud objections of her mother, divorced herself, and her two brothers who were friends with Joe, Jane flew to Reno to establish her six-week residency that would allow her the dignity of an uncontested divorce.

Her flight to Nevada seemed a matter of expediency. Jane thought space, not time, would heal all wounds, and Nevada offered plenty of that. Still, it frightened her how easy it was to get over Joseph. She had expected to be devastated. Instead, she was relieved, not only from the burden of him but from her family as well. From their anticipations. The only time Jane felt bad was whenever one of them called. It wasn't their words that made her ache but the thick pauses in between.

For a while she fretted over her repose, wondered if the speed of her recovery made her a shallow person. But the greater realization, the one that washed over all others, was the sense that she had situated herself perfectly. Here was a state big enough to hide her. A city that offered both opportunity and anonymity, the perfect combination. She found work at the first place she applied although not for the misses dresses position she sought. "No offense, but you don't strike me as a closer," the floor manager told her and offered her the fragrance model position instead. That was three years ago.

And though her mother disbelieved her, Jane did like her job. Not her fellow employees so much who, except for Hal and Morris in men's suits, seemed self-possessed, and who, in turn, found Jane cold and distant, a realization that prompted Jane to assume a veneer of courtesy that no one would mistake for friendship. She liked the pay. And most of the fragrances even though they left her hands permanently scented. And the customers because they remained curious strangers. She liked the ones who immediately said yes to her offer of application, those willing to do something impulsive, risk improvement. And the ones who needed prodding, compelling evidence that they were doing something worthwhile. These timid souls Jane sprayed lightly, a cat sneeze, she told them, then waited for them to surrender the other wrist. She even liked the skeptical ones who hurriedly rubbed in the wetness, then sniffed as if tasting wine, anxious to render judgment. Most of all, she liked the ones who cast nervous glances as if they were doing something naughty before quickly accepting a spritz and just as quickly disappearing. They seemed bulimic with desire.

At least the women did. The men were another matter. The men who let her spray them weren't shy; they were sneaky. Or chagrined, as if smelling good was wrong. Or brazen, not there for a hit of cologne but to hit on her.

JANE PULLED HER HONDA CIVIC *"It looks like a pillbox," her mother had said on her only visit to Reno, a three day disaster. "Why can't you drive something bigger? Something American?"*

into the far corner lot reserved for Burton's employees. She remembered the tomcat, its look of annoyance, as if she were the one who had breached decorum. Those were the customers Jane detested, the men who stopped just beyond the point of approach and glared at her, forcing her to smile in this game of chicken, to step aside. They behaved as if only their lives held purpose.

This notion of territory bothered her. The last time she'd been in a bar *two years ago?* she'd forfeited her seat to a man who claimed it as rightfully his. In tears she'd run out, abandoning a full drink. It was as if every man thought of himself as a country, as if each one had the right to designate his own sovereignty, codify his own indignations. They were all border guards, Jane decided, caged dogs desperate for something to defend. Like the two stock boys she'd seen fighting over a parking space though there were other available spaces close by. Like Cheswick, who always referred to cosmetics as *my* department. Or Joseph, always demanding space, then sulking when he got it. Joseph, who made her realize that it wasn't free range men sought, but rather, the fence around it. And the safety behind these fences. And the fear that made them, him, so willing to defend the things that should have belonged to no one.

TODAY'S THE DAY, JANE REMINDED herself as she punched her time card. In the employee restroom, she ran a quick brush through her hair and adjusted her pantyhose before bracing herself for her final day of work.

"You're working men's wear!" Pam told her before she had a chance to scan the assignment roster. Jane set her purse underneath the Clinique counter, felt around for the silver tray and that day's atomizer. *Brut* she saw written beside her name. She rummaged through the box of opened sampler fragrances, annoyed that she would be offering such a pedestrian scent on such an important day.

"Want to trade shifts?" Pam asked. "I could ask Mr. Cheswick."

Jane smiled stiffly, brushed back her hair, decided not to tell Pam how close she was to being granted her wish.

Men's wear was oddly void of the morning wives shopping for their husbands. The men, the ones who would be anointed with Brut on this red letter day, *"Brut! Why don't I just hose them down with beer?" she had wanted to ask Cheswick the last time Brut was the selected scent* wouldn't come until lunch, until boredom or hunger drove them from their offices. Jane nodded to Morris and Hal who both stood, arms folded, by the cash register. She liked these two because they didn't fluff up shirts or otherwise pretend to be busy for Cheswick's sake. And because neither of them hit on her.

"What are you offering today?"

The man's voice startled her. "Brut," she said. "By Fabrege. Try some?"

"I will if you'll have lunch with me."

"I can't," Jane said. "Brut?"

"No, but I'd like to be."

She scanned him, unable to light on anything. She retreated to the suit racks to an elderly couple. "Brut. By Fabrege," she said to the man, disregarding his wife's skepticism. "Care to try some?" And before he replied, she spritzed one of his wrists. She sensed the first man following her, gave the grateful older man a second application, saw that she was spraying his watch, turned, saw her pursuer fifteen feet away, holding silk ties like reins, his eyes fixed on her.

Jane set down her tray atop a shirt display, held her decanter in front of her stiff-armed as if it were a cross, and walked slowly, unveeringly, toward him.

"Brut," she said. "Brut on brute," and sprayed the man's chest.

"My shirt!"

"Et tu, Brut," she said and sprayed him again.

The man shot her a menacing look but retreated. Jane drew a distaff in his direction. She went to retrieve her tray and saw Hal and Morris applauding. Then she did something she promised herself to stop doing. She cried.

She would give notice as soon as Cheswick appeared.

That's the scenario Jane imagined as she retreated from her admirer. The truth was, rage and hurt and conviction were all colors she had removed from her emotional palette. It would take a while to restore them. She searched for someone else to spray. She felt like one of her spritzes, her anger already dissipating.

PERCHED ON THE RIM of the mall fountain, nibbling on a pita bread sandwich, she watched the passing shoppers as if regarding another species. The women, plainly unhappy, tethered by their wandering, curious children. The men who clutched the throats of their plastic shopping bags as if they were transporting toxic waste. The teenage girls there for the scene, not the sale. Their male counterparts in black tee shirts and turned baseball caps, desperately indifferent, lurking in the tortuous gap between their desires and their courage.

It was this last group that drew her attention. Three of them stood outside the door of a women's apparel store, extending out in single file. They formed a human dam that forced the other shoppers to walk around them. Whether they realized this or not, Jane couldn't tell. Then it dawned on her. She rested her sandwich on the wax paper napkin in her lap, marveling at this latest notion. Men had this territory thing all wrong. Establishing one's turf, marking stationary objects, was too limiting. Too final. It didn't allow for growth. For expansion.

"I want more," Jane said aloud.

"What?" asked a passing woman who thought Jane was speaking to her.

"I want more," Jane told her. The woman smiled but kept moving.

Jane returned to work five minutes early. Cheswick had finally appeared, displeased as always, but for once Jane didn't blame herself for his ill temper. She greeted him warmly, giddy with her discovery. Already, there were a dozen human markers from this morning floating out somewhere in Reno, expanding *her* turf. She traded her purse for the decanter and tray. Quitting was now out of the question. And to prove it, she sprayed herself, rubbed her wrists together, breathed deeply, then sprayed the air around her. "Brut," she said. "Fabrege's finest."

A new approach was manifest. If men were to be the stakes of her territory, *but that wasn't it; this wasn't a matter of staking out land but charting undiscovered seas, dropping buoys, letting them drift away randomly to their natural destinations. Boys will be buoys. Oh! This was all so marvelous!* then she needed to mark as many men as possible. In the past, she had relied on instinctively knowing which customers were willing to succumb to her spray and listen to her spiel. She knew better than to approach any married man over forty without approval from his wife. Or any professional woman whose scrupulously coordinated outfit would surely include a matching scent. In the past, she situated herself in popular but uncrowded aisles and waited for customers to approach her. The trick was to let them think it was their choice.

No more. Jane now moved to wherever men were browsing even if it meant crossing over into women's wear. "Brut?" she asked.

The choice was theirs. Either a man accepted her invitation and became one of her buoys, or Jane marked their backs with a full spritz as they retreated.

She wondered when the moment of discovery would occur for the unwilling ones. Would they catch full wind of themselves once inside their cars? Or would it happen later, while crossing Donner Summit into California, or outside Hawthorne on the way to Vegas, their dull senses finally aroused? She saw them spreading in all directions, her dominion a tide that flowed in all directions. Would it be when they returned to their offices? Would someone else notice it first? Their secretaries? Their wives?

All afternoon, she sprayed Brut on every man who crossed her path except for Morris and Hal. For four hours, she forgot about her pinching shoes, her do-nothing hair, Pam's envy, Cheswick, Joseph, her mother, quitting. Today, the world had gotten bigger. It now carried beyond the walls of Burton's, beyond the state line, PST, the empty side of her bed. It wasn't until Hal said, "Come to your senses," as he did each day at five, their private pun, that Jane realized her shift was over. And it wasn't until she reached the employee parking lot where again she had to pass some guy's beat up Bonneville with the LAY DOWN - I THINK I LOVE YOU and I BRAKE FOR 16 YEAR OLDS bumper stickers that Jane regretted not bringing her atomizer with her.

SHE LAUGHED WHEN THE LIZ CLAIBORNE rep asked Jane if she could dispense the entire liter of Revealment in a week's time. Since Jane had begun her quest, it had been difficult not to exhaust the daily ration. The real difficulty lay in days like this when she was assigned a women's line. Since interloping into men's wear would surely draw attention, Jane expanded her mission. She still misted all men who passed through the women's section, but now, certain women as well. Women who acted like men. Bossy women. Abrupt women. Indignant women.

The reluctance of some customers, especially the ones who flashed that look that was supposed to make her feel like she was peddling smut, now delighted her. Her joy surprised Cheswick, froze him long enough for Jane to spray the elbow of his linen suit. Pam she hit with two full applications, one on each buttock. And again at lunchtime, she marked Pam for sulking about her job. But as Jane felt below the counter for her purse, she noticed Pam's puffy ankles and feet and wondered if she needed to be more selective in designating her buoys.

At the food pavilion, she told herself she wasn't being snobby. Her mother was the snob. The saleswomen at Burton's who Pam said referred to Jane as *The Cube* were wrong. She wasn't aloof; she was lonely, not for friendship but for companionship, something she found impossible to confess.

How could she? It was admitting to being a social leper, personally inept, and worst of all, reliant. She had tried. Initially, she attended the baby showers and the Friday night cocktail hours that she quickly found incestuously stifling.

And male free. By herself, she had frequented the casinos but found the men there more interested in their cards. She had even considered placing a personal ad in the

Gazette-Journal but disliked the idea of reducing her very existence to a series of acronyms. The ad she reworked for an hour didn't fill the minimum four lines.

So she braved it. She stopped answering Joseph's late night calls. She let her correspondence with college friends lapse. She wrote but no longer telephoned her family. She stopped attending Burton's functions and soon, the saleswomen stopped inviting her. At work, she always kept her tray between herself and everyone else. It wasn't a matter of elitism or resentment. She didn't blame them. She didn't blame anyone. She had tried and failed; she deserved her quarantine.

INSTEAD OF ASSUMING HER NORMAL spot by the fountain, Jane ate as she walked. She searched the aisles of three toy stores until she found the perfect dispenser: a four-dollar black, plastic, Luger-shaped water pistol guaranteed by the manufacturer to be leak proof. She refused the clerk's offer of a bag. She dropped her receipt on the counter, kept those in line behind her waiting while she ripped the pistol free from its plastic wrapper. She felt the heft of the pistol which, even empty, seemed heavy.

She knew the afternoon would be a long one. Avoiding customers was more work than serving them. When possible, Jane drifted into men's wear to becalm Morris, upset about Hal's latest ailment. At shift's end, careful not to spill, she crouched down behind the Clinique counter and emptied the last four ounces of Revealment into the pistol.

SHE SOAKED HER HANDS an extra five minutes in the warm, soapy water she knew did little to remove the perpetual stench. Still, it was important that tonight she carry no scent.

After all, she was the buoy maker, not a buoy. Jane made herself a salad and a bagel but was too excited to eat much of either. She left the remnants of her dinner on the table and ran to her closet for her clingy peasant dress and matching pumps and purse.

The first bar proved too easy. Perhaps it was her outfit or that the long bar that ran against the wall restricted movement, but marking men inside this place was like painting a wall. Because it was Friday and crowded, the men stood too close for her to squeeze off a full round. Jane slipped the pistol inside her clutch purse and walked into the twilight down Virginia Street. The last time she had felt this good was when she had walked out of the Washoe County courthouse she was now passing. Walked out waving her divorce decree like a diploma, resolute that she had learned something valuable. Jane stared at the courthouse. She wondered where her file was stored. She had the urge to mark it.

By the post office, she squeezed a shot into each drive-up mailbox. Outside the Club Cal-Neva, she aimed her gun skyward at the jutting jaw of the Nevada-headed cowboy and listened to the neon sizzle. She was now certain of her aim.

Inside the Money Mountain, she shot the marquee poster of Evander Holyfield. She heard a 21 player say "Hit me," and did. From ten feet away, she marked three craps dealers who stood disinterested over a dead game. Then marked their pit boss. In another part of the club, she tagged a disgruntled player she heard tell a pit boss, "I need a marker," even after the man had turned to size her up. Jane sensed that her shift from sight to smell made her invisible to everyone she passed—and marked.

She shot the jack of hearts, the end card of a deck spread across a 21 game. She shot a roulette ball. She shot Willie

Nelson coming out an alley exit door. She shot a security guard in the crotch, certain that he'd felt the hit.

Always, her animate targets were men. The pudgy ones, pudding inside their clothes. The married ones who cast Jane furtive looks when they thought their wives weren't looking. The cowboys who wore broken smiles. And especially the groups of men, conventioneers, businessmen, softball teams, so secure in their sameness, certain that the world held one true vision, theirs, always oozing confidence that allowed them to stare at women for as long as they cared.

Jane emptied her gun on a group who wore matching tee shirts that said *The Elbow Room* then walked next door to the Aces Oasis casino. She sat at the bar, disappointed that she'd run out of Revealment so soon. Hands folded neatly in front of her, she ordered a drink. She considered buying more perfume at the casino's gift shop, but the thought of paying for perfume seemed as abhorrent as the scent that had leaked after all onto her trigger finger.

"Can you settle a bet?"

Jane frowned at the man standing beside her, angry with him for startling her. He wore blacks and whites, casino garb. She guessed that he was a dealer, probably her age.

"I've got a hundred dollars that says you're not a hooker."

Jane reached for her daiquiri. "Go away. Please." She glanced at his name tag, saw that his name was Essex, that his hometown was San Jose, California.

"I'm serious," he said. "Dead Bob bet me a bill we'd go a month without finding a single woman at the bar who wasn't working. I just bet him another hundred that you're the one. Are you?"

Jane grabbed her bag, made her way for the door.

"I *am* right!" she heard him say.

At home, she took off her dress and shoes and onyx necklace and put on her kimono. She fished the pistol from her handbag, and in front of her hallway mirror, fired off imaginary rounds while twisting and turning in secret agent poses. She shot at imaginary targets. At that dealer, Essex.

She heard a ruckus outside her bedroom window, two cats yowling. Were they fighting or mating? She loaded her pistol with tap water, then stole to the sliding door. She raised her gun, ready, but the noise had ceased.

In the dining room alcove, she saw the meal she'd left at the table. Jane wondered momentarily if she had a roommate. She tucked her gun inside the sash of her kimono, poured herself a glass of ice tea, sat down to eat. The fright Essex had given her couldn't negate the feeling that, finally, her life had intent. She heard the cats resume their shrieking.

WHEN SHE FIRST BEGAN AT BURTON'S, Jane was instructed to tell customers that certain scents were suited for certain people. She now believed this to be true. At night, she let whatever perfume or cologne she'd been hawking that day, whatever scent she'd filled her pistol with when nosy Pam wasn't around, determine whom she'd mark. Loaded with Obsession, she sought men who seemed too intent on winning. Or wooing. Anyone who seemed to love the game beyond the prize. Armed with Canoe, she searched for men in Top-Siders or men sporting Navy tattoos. Guys who acted like they were on leave.

Wonderment about that day's scent drew her to work early. She spurned invitations from several saleswomen to join their circle at lunch. "Are you seeing someone?" one of them asked. Cheswick gave her a raise. Only Morris and

Hal disapproved of the new Jane after they discovered she was buying a new dress every payday.

"You're becoming one of them," Morris told her. Jane shrugged, secretly hoping that Cheswick would find her new indigo sundress too flippant for floor wear. She wanted to be noticed. Last night, even in her red silk dress and three-inch heels, she had felt invisible. Not safe but small. Her mother, who called just after Jane had returned from marking patrons at the Meadowood Mall, had asked her to speak up, told her she wasn't projecting.

Weekends, when she had no access to floor samples, posed a problem. Jane thought about loading up during the week, but that seemed premeditated. Plus it would force her, not fate, to decide what sort of person got marked. Weekends also failed to provide much distraction. She did much better when there wasn't time to think about things. On most Saturdays, she tried to lose herself in a book until twilight, when she would eat sparingly, take a long, hot shower, fix her hair, put on a dress and heels, then stop at K-Mart for her weekend supply of scent. Spontaneity came in whatever was on sale, always a prosaic fragrance that fit the weekend crowd she found less exotic.

But everything was becoming less exotic because the more reckless Jane became, the more invisible she seemed to become. The topper had been shooting players' hands from the balcony above the pit main in the Money Mountain Casino. When no one noticed, she began spraying indiscriminately, even women, sending a fine shower over several tables as if she were misting houseplants. For the first time, Jane quit before emptying her pistol.

Over her nightcap daiquiri at the Aces Oasis, she realized the game would soon be over. Marking a man's skin or short-sleeved shirt had always been the allure. But now that it was October, many of them had begun wearing sweaters and overcoats. And it seemed, perhaps from the crack by the trigger, that she had also marked herself, become one of them. These past few weeks, she had found herself becoming less offended by the men who invited her to have a drink. She found herself less amused by the ones who approached her nervously, who wore their trepidation like a medical alert bracelet. Their pitch exposed everything about them. They were sausages without skins. But what upset Jane most was realizing that if she knew what to say, it might be *Yes*.

SHE HOPED IT WASN'T HER SNIFFLING that had attracted him. Even with Joseph, she had never used her emotions as bait. But tonight, it had all come down. Maybe the phone call from Alice, who never called on Saturday night, should have served as a warning. Her news, that Joseph's second wife had also dumped him, didn't cheer her up. She didn't reply when her mother said, "What goes around comes around." If Jane had, she would have said, "What goes around just keeps going."

Alice told her about the airplane fare wars, said she could fly from Reno to Boston for a hundred dollars.

"That's only one way," Jane reminded her.

"Exactly."

Jane told her mother she was going to a play and needed to get ready, but after she hung up, Jane sat still for some time. The news about Joseph wasn't good. She didn't feel vindicated; she felt common. Now she was merely part of a pattern. When she finally did stir, it was to her closet in search of her most provocative dress.

Tonight, she had gotten caught in Lucky's Club. An hour after putting on the backless number, some hairy man in an open jumpsuit whose medallion she'd hit dead on from ten feet had turned, caught her eye, wiped the icon dry, held it to his nose, smiled appreciatively. Said "Thank you, Venus." Then grabbed Jane by the wrist, forced her to assume a seat beside him at a 21 table.

"Stay and play or I'll tell Security," the man said. He increased all three of his bets. "My name's Marvin," he said and scratched for a hit on his third hand. "What's yours?"

"Pam."

The man won all three hands. This time, he left his bets alone. "Pleased to meet you, Pam," he said, turning his first hand over, then his second, then the third. "Look at this," he announced to the dealer. "Three double downs." Marvin watched as the dealer dealt a queen to all three hands. "Look at that!" he said. "Six tits!"

The dealer busted her own hand, feigned delight, cast a fleeting glare at Jane who saw in her the eyes of Joseph's second wife. Another round of cards exhausted the shoe. The dealer now began reshuffling the six decks.

Marvin threw one hirsute arm around his chips, the other around Jane. "You and me are in for a night," he said, then to the dealer, "I want to buy back my marker." He lobbed a hundred-dollar chip to the dealer, held another one up for Jane.

Jane reddened. "I don't want your money," she said. "I'm not a prostitute."

"I know," Marvin said. "You're Annie Oakley. Hey, they're made out of clay. Use it for target practice." He placed the chip in Jane's palm, folded her fingers around it. "You have nice hands," he told her.

Jane thought about reaching for her pistol, saw a pit boss approaching their table with a slip of paper for Marvin to sign. She knew he wasn't about to abandon his money, so she bolted.

"THANK YOU," JANE SAID WHEN the bartender at the Aces Oasis asked if she'd like another drink. Normally, it was one and done. But the memory of that man, his gratitude and his greed, was proving difficult to erase. She reached into her red leather satchel for another Kleenex and felt the bulk of her nearly full squirt gun. She hoped the man behind her *Was Essex his name?* would leave, wouldn't see her shivering with dread. Why couldn't memory become invisible?

"How are you?" she heard him ask again.

"Fine."

"Haven't seen you in a while."

"Haven't been myself in a while," she said, feeling her blush.

"I was wrong about you. You're not a tourist. Dead Bob paid me off, but I never spent the money. I carry it on me. Here."

Jane reached instead for her drink.

"Don't!" he said, and Jane realized that he had expected her to douse him with her drink. She smiled, astonished that she could instill fear.

He sat down beside her, showed her two one-hundred-dollar bills. "Come on," he said. "You've got to help me spend these. They're yours, too, you know."

"There you are!" a voice behind them beckoned. Jane spun around on her stool, saw that it was Marvin, leering, holding his medallion to his nose and smiling, but only briefly before retreating, crestfallen, into the dissonant crowd. Jane stared, puzzled, until she realized that Essex was standing, fists clenched.

She watched him ease his grip, remove his name tag and clip-on tie. "I'm sorry," he said. "I had no right to do that."

Jane stood, slid her arm through his, told him her name was Alice. She could still feel the prick of her blush that she understood to be a sign of visibility. He was moving them to another casino lounge, a more private one, but Jane didn't mind. It would provide safe haven from men like Marvin who honored turf.

For two hours, they talked. Essex wanted them to play 21, but she had him teach her how to play keno. He kept the money *their money* spread out on the round Formica table. He never touched it, allowing the keno runners and cocktail waitresses to make all transactions. "Take a little for yourself," he told them each time and purposely, for her sake Jane thought, did not notice what they took.

He told her about himself. What it was like growing up in "San Jose, the Lost City of America," always an hour away from something better. He told her that he'd dreamed of being a basketball player but had stopped growing. That he hoped to travel, live in the real world, raise a family.

"So you don't like being a dealer?"

He slapped a soggy dollar around each wrist, held them out like handcuffs. "I'm like every dealer. I hate my job. I hate this town. I make too much to leave."

"How are you not like every dealer?" She watched his lip quiver. It was cute.

"I've found someone who doesn't work in the clubs," he said. "Finally. Someone who has a life of her own. Hell, somebody who has a life." He considered Jane. "At least I think you do." He drained his drink, asked her up to his place.

Jane brought her hands to her face, again felt the heat. She looked at the pile of wet money, at the keno board, at him. She drew closer to him, not for affection but to smell him. To make sure he wasn't wearing cologne.

HE WANTED TO DRIVE HER, but she insisted on following him in her car, up Keystone Avenue to his home on Mormon Hill above King's Row. She stared hard at herself in her rear view mirror, wondering if she looked as nervous as she felt. Tonight, she would do just that—sleep with him. No giving in. Just sleep. It would be enough to know that someone was occupying the space beside her. Later on, if things felt right, she would let more out. Tell him the things he seemed to want to know. Where she worked. What she did. Whether she too hated her job. Why someone like her was unattached. In due time, she would tell him her name.

She parked her car in the driveway beside his car. It reminded her of the driveway she and Joseph had shared. Same incline. Same his and her spaces, her spot further from the door. She grabbed her satchel, hoped it wasn't shaking noticeably.

She found him in the kitchen, rummaging through his appliances, apologizing for being unable to make her a daiquiri. "I don't want one," she said. "Do you have ice tea?" She liked him for not wanting to embrace her. For not checking his blinking phone messages.

He brought her a glass of tea with a straw and as an afterthought, cut her a lemon wedge. "Take a look around," he said, excusing himself. "Admire. Dust."

The tea did little to unclench her tightening throat. She paced through the living room and sun porch deciding how she would decorate the place. She suddenly felt foolish to be wearing a dress and pearls.

He seemed to be gone a long time. She sat down on the edge of his couch, placed her dewy glass on a magazine. She thought about leaving. She rose to leave her glass in the kitchen, heard footsteps, traced the little beads of water around her glass that felt like sweat.

"Sorry," he said. "I got distracted." Jane frowned but she was glad that he hadn't changed out of his clothes into something casual or committal. She let him kiss her, then wondered if she'd broken away too soon. It had been too long. She had lost her timing. She would have to rely on his.

"Let me take you for a tour," he said and took her hand. The floor plan and decor held no surprises, yet he seemed to find something in each room worth describing, as if these things weren't apparent to her. Jane couldn't decide if she was being charmed or patronized.

One thing was certain. This was all leading to his bedroom where he sat her down on his bed, then sat beside her. "Feel this," he said and brought her hand to his chest. "Drums along the Mohawk. I can't believe I'm this nervous."

Jane didn't care if it was a line. Tonight was a small concession to something bigger. Tonight, one of her markers had come to rest.

"You're the first person I've invited here," he said. "I know that sounds like a lie, but my home is important to me. I don't let delivery drivers step inside." Again they kissed. Jane sat so rigidly, her spine hurt.

Abruptly, he released her and snapped his fingers. "I almost forgot," he said. "Be right back."

Jane eased off her shoes. She removed her necklace and earrings, placing them on the bed stand she guessed would be hers. She walked over to his bureau and opened several drawers until she found a Bass Pro Shop tee shirt big enough to be a nightie.

The wall was thin enough for her to hear him talking in the room next door, the one he had called his headquarters. She heard him laughing. Jane crumpled up the tee shirt and flung it into a corner before stealing up to the doorway of his den. "Yep. Yep," she heard him say. "Hey, that's two C notes already. Double or nothing? Okay, stay in the soak cycle; I don't care. Sure. That's what the video is for. No, I'm not going to tell her. Christ, would you? Four hundred it is, the price of rice."

It took her only a moment to find the video recorder nestled in the thick Boston fern that hung by his closet. It took just a moment longer to wedge into her shoes and throw her earrings and necklace into her satchel where she felt the barrel of her water pistol.

She hid in the corner behind the door. When he entered, she waited until he called out her name, "Alice. Alice?" then shot him squarely in each eye.

"Brut!" she shouted and fired again, bringing him to his knees as he tried to scratch the alcohol from his eyes. "Ambush!" she shouted and fired a round of Babe into his twisted mouth. "Poison!" "Tabu!" "That Man!" She began dousing his crotch with the last of the pistol's reserve. "Fire and Ice," she shouted, waving her pistol at the camera. "Fire and Ice!"

She expected to be struck. Instead, he ran away from her to the bathroom sink, which gave her just enough time to raise her skirt, lower her panties, and mark the door to his headquarters.

JANE LET HER DRESS AND SLIP lay where she had gotten out of them. There would be time to put everything away. She thought about calling Alice just because she never called her mother this time of day, but for now, Jane was content to sit on the edge of her bed and sip lemon water.

Already, the sun was rising, affording everything depth and shade. She rose only to drop the water pistol into a waste basket. She felt the sun on her back, watched her shadow extend across the floor. Today was a work day, but Jane was uncertain if she would. She would let the coming light decide all matters of distance.

SAND SHARK

In Reno this morning, Davitz packed his work clothes in one suitcase, the rest of his belongings in another and took off, not bothering to notify his landlord or the rental furniture company. It didn't dawn on him until he passed Lovelock that the Blazing Banjo might be one of those casinos where the dealers wore cowboy clothes. He wasn't put off when Hedderly pressed half a dozen drink tokens in his palm and told him to wait at the bar. He assumed that as the Banjo's new GM, it was necessary for Hedderly to visibly sweat the money whenever a table was dumping. He wondered what constituted big money in a club like this.

Davitz circled the casino, disappointed by its smallness, the color of the dice *lavender!*, the lack of attractive 21 dealers, but he resolved to work here just the same. At least the dealers wore black and whites. He knew that in the spring there would be jobs again in Reno. By that time, people would have forgotten.

At the bar, Davitz settled for a Henry's because they didn't stock any microbeers. He slid one of Hedderly's drink tokens and a silver dollar toward the bartender who asked him if he wanted a glass. "Comes in a glass, doesn't it?" Davitz said. He ignored the bartender's muddle. Instead, he watched the cocktail waitresses milling around their station, a sure sign that there were no money players in the club. Behind them, he saw half a drum set resting on a barren stage. Davitz covered the poker machine screen in front of him with bar napkins. "Lose-emucca," he said to himself, laughed, studied his manicured hands that he knew this town did not deserve.

"Sorry, Mike," Hedderly said and drew up a stool beside him. "Coffee, please, Lenny," he told the bartender in a clipped Jersey accent that a decade in Nevada had not honed. He clapped Davitz on the back. "So where are you heading?"

"Here."

"Yeah, right. Number One in Winnemucca. There's an image."

"I'm serious," Davitz said.

"I'm hungry. Are you?" Hedderly didn't wait for a reply. He endorsed the receipt by his coffee mug, led Davitz to the only restaurant in the casino where he again slapped him on the back. "Man, it's good to see someone from civilization."

The hostess took them to a booth exclusively reserved for Hedderly, who periodically begged off to converse with customers. Davitz noticed that most of the restaurant staff made a point to catch Ricky's eye to nod their hellos. He decided that their waitress, who bore three small crucifix tattoos on her fingers but no rings, was prettier than any of the dealers, and that her service, she never allowed their coffee cups to empty more than an inch, was not just for Hedderly's sake.

"So tell me what happened at the Aces," Hedderly said when they were halfway into their meals. "I've heard all the rumors. I want to hear it from you."

Davitz stiffened from the cracked vinyl that was jabbing his shoulder. He and Hedderly went back all the way to craps school at the Money Mountain, but Ricky was now a suit. Davitz was unsure whether to tell him the dealer or the pit boss version.

"Ed Wooten," he said coolly, but Hedderly didn't budge. "I refused to pay him for a late bet."

"That doesn't get you fired," Hedderly said. "Who'd you really piss off?"

He saw Hedderly squirming not from the conversation but from his failure to gain their waitress's attention who reappeared a minute later from their blind side carrying three slices of cherry pie they hadn't ordered. Two of them she placed in front of Hedderly. "You're aces, Faydene," Hedderly said which made her blush.

"Were the purple dice your idea?" Davitz asked.

"You're not going to tell me, are you?"

Davitz did. He recounted the clumsiness of Wooten's late bet, his indignation, how the floorman, Sherwood, first placated the player, then cut out the money himself, six one-hundred-dollar chips, when Davitz refused to do it. He told Hedderly how Max and Dead Bob, his crewmates, gaped in disbelief when he responded to Sherwood's tapping his hand in an attempt to gain his attention by sending the chips flying across the layout with a flick of the offended wrist.

"I didn't mean to make such a mess," Davitz said, which got Hedderly snorting with laughter. "But the idea of Sherwood touching me creeped me out."

"I guess so!"

Davitz put down his fork. "I need a job, Ricky, just for the winter."

"What you need," Hedderly said, "is to keep heading east until you reach grass. You got the message; now hang up the phone."

"Just work me for six months."

"Can't do it. In fact, you're persona non grata at all Megastar casinos. I'm supposed to be giving you the royal boot, not comping you to a meal. Sorry, buddy."

"What about the other clubs here?"

Hedderly reached for his second piece of pie. "Still the shark, aren't you?"

"How can you turn down these hands?" Davitz held them out like a surgeon awaiting sanitaries. "Six months. That's it. Come on, Ricky."

"This isn't your kind of town, Mike. I doubt if Scottie or Alan have any spots open anyway. It's November for Christ's sake. Tell you what, though. If it's a room you need. Or money—" Hedderly waited for Davitz to look at him. "That sort of thing I can do."

Davitz shook his head. He'd accept the meal but only because the casino, not Hedderly, was paying for it. He hadn't driven a hundred and sixty miles just to pick Hedderly's pocket. Over coffee, they talked about mutual friends, chukker hunting, the new golf course that Hedderly wasn't getting out to. Hedderly wanted to know who now had AIDS. They talked until Hedderly grew uneasy about being away from his responsibilities. Davitz insisted on leaving the tip and dug into his pocket for loose silver dollars. He felt one of Hedderly's drink tokens slip out. He dug again and slipped the rest of them onto the carpet.

He said nothing when Hedderly pounded him on the back a final time before lighting out to the bigger of the two pits. Davitz walked the other way, saw a 21 dealer flash him her biggest smile. He did not smile back.

Maybe he should have backed down, Davitz wondered on the way to his car, just played along like Brennan and his shift boss had asked him to do. He didn't tell Hedderly that upstairs in the pit office, they had advised him to accept the write-up, to take his week on the street like a man, to apologize to Sherwood.

"Let me see if I'm getting this right," Davitz said. "We reward cheaters."

"It's not *your* money," Brennan told him.

"No," Davitz bristled, "just my reputation."

"And your career," his shifter added.

At the time, he thought Brennan was the one who had made the mistake, letting in Sherwood, who had been waiting outside for his apology. Still, it wasn't Sherwood's look of umbrage that pushed Davitz's needle past the red zone; it was his puffy, sweaty hands. Once he caught sight of those greasy sausage fingers that seemed more suited for deep frying than cutting chips, Davitz grew incensed. This centipede had no right to convey orders, let alone touch hands that had forgotten more moves than Sherwood had ever learned. So Davitz rose, asked when he was due to report back to work, left without speaking to Sherwood.

When his suspension was lifted a week later, Davitz was summoned to the pit office and fired. That was yesterday.

DAVITZ PUSHED HIS COROLLA far beyond the legal seventy per. He wanted to get to the Elko casinos while their personnel offices were still open, before swing shift began when it would be too busy for him to audition. He crushed the last of a joint, rolled it into a ball, tossed it out the window. He laughed, wondering why he'd bothered snuffing the ember. There was nothing out there to burn. In front of him, beyond the rust and khaki-colored hills that seemed pure backdrop, the sun was falling. Davitz crossed a dry lake and looked for signs of life, a hawk, a cloud, drain ditch water, roadkill, anything that could prove to him he wasn't the only source of life out here.

This stretch of desert, his windshield, the absence of motion—all of it reminded him of the reptile tank he maintained as a boy even after his mother refused to buy him any more lizards after the third one died just like the others, after shedding its skin. The glass case became nothing more than a box of sand and rock, but Davitz had steadfastly insisted on keeping it in his room. He thought that some sort of lizard, a Gila Monster maybe, would appear someday on his window sill, but it never happened.

He plugged in a new cassette, cursed Hedderly, recalled working at the Money Mountain, his first and longest dealing job. Two years he'd dealt craps there, six months with Hedderly, all undone by his dressing down of a new boxman in front of another pit boss. That this flea had no business boxing a craps game wasn't the point. That a dealer had no cause to insult a suit was.

Afterward, he shared a drink with his three crewmates at the most visible bar in the club, but only Hedderly lingered. "You're a Nevada sand shark," Hedderly kept repeating. "A goddamn sand shark. You're the one making all those lines in the desert sand." They drank Kamikazes. They drank until they could sense from their windowless vantage point the sun rising. Then they walked to their cars while Hedderly lamented the break-up of their crew. "How could they fire you? You've got the best hands in the state. Numero Uno."

"And you've got the hands of a sturgeon," Davitz said. "Hands like feet."

"You'll survive," Hedderly averred. "Sharks can only go forward."

HE COULDN'T SEE IT, BUT AS HE descended Echo Pass, Davitz was certain that a big E made of whitewashed stones loomed somewhere above him on one of the surrounding foothills. Today, he had driven past the L above Lovelock, the I above Imlay, Valmy's V, the BM above Battle Mountain where Davitz muttered, "You got that right." He wondered why these towns took such pride in these markers. What was the point? Were the locals afraid they wouldn't be able to distinguish their town from the tumbleweeds? Or from other towns? Were these stone monograms the only thing preventing these places from being blown away when the afternoon zephyrs ripped through? Each town Davitz had passed today seemed like a mistake. Their scraggly tree lines seemed nothing more than grass escaping through cracks in a sidewalk. He didn't get it. Perseverance and pride seemed miles apart.

Davitz drove up and down the strip scoping out suitable places. The warning light had been on since Carlin, but gas would have to wait. Instead, he drove into the crowded parking lot of the Cartwheel Casino right up to the empty space by the main entrance. Davitz took this as a good sign. Purposely, he didn't look around for a handicapped marker, focusing instead on his reflection in the rear view mirror. He ran a comb through his hair and a finger across his teeth before popping a Certs into his mouth and grabbing a sports coat from the back seat.

What he really wanted was a beer, but Davitz veered for the biggest pit, scanned the pit stand, decided that the bald man in the Pendleton sports jacket, the one who looked like that comic, Gallagher, was likely the shifter. He passed a row of half busy 21 tables, nodded confidently at the one craps crew that stood bored over their dead game, walked right up to the pit stand, surprised that he could get this far without obstruction.

"My name is Michael Davitz," he announced to the three pit bosses clustered there. "I'm a craps dealer looking for work." He looked each of them, Winken, Blinken, and Nod, squarely in the eye. The one he assumed to be the shifter was the only one who extended his hand.

"Craig Deaton."

"I'd like to come work for you, Craig," Davitz said. "If you let me audition for you, I'm sure you'll sign me on."

"Sorry, I've already got a dozen part-timers I can't find enough work for."

"But you haven't seen me deal," Davitz said.

"There's a lot of things I haven't seen," Deaton said, "including my wife for the last three days. You have yourself a nice day." He turned his attention to a carton of unopened decks.

Davitz lingered momentarily, just to let him, them, know the kind of person they were passing up. As he passed the gauntlet of 21 dealers, he looked intently into each of their faces, not looking ahead until each one met his gaze. Austin, Davitz guessed. Fallon. Beowawe. Elko. Again, he thought about a beer, decided this club didn't deserve his business.

At the Golden Spike, he didn't bother approaching anyone. It was shift change. Everyone wearing a suit was busy assigning the swing shift dealers a table or helping security replace the drop boxes on each game. Davitz decided he'd eat, gas up, get a room, shower, return when things got settled.

Outside, he avoided the gaze of three cowboys who gave him an extended *dude* look. Little men with big friends, he thought. Like Sherwood. They're the ones to avoid.

He took up another casino's offer of a sixteen-ounce T-bone for $5.95 and after his third beer—apparently no one out here carried microbrews—decided to play a little 21. Purposely, he didn't scan the tables for the most attractive or least jaded dealer but assumed a seat at the table closest to the restaurant. He bought in for a twenty that he turned into three hundred dollars in four beers' time because the dealer was unwittingly exposing her hole card. At first, her ineptitude made him nervous. Was she doing it intentionally? Then Davitz realized how lax game security was this far off the beaten track. It would be easy, he decided, dealing in one of these joints.

Normally, he was a conspicuous tipper, but since no one knew him here, Davitz tipped the dealer just ten dollars, took the rest to the cashiers' cage where the chips in his left hand spilled across the counter.

"How would you like this?" asked the cashier. She reminded Davitz of a young Dale Evans.

"In pennies, please."

"Oh no, we don't have penny slots anymore."

Davitz smiled, told her hundreds would do just fine. That's going to be the hard part, he thought, finding conversation.

THE CRISP NIGHT AIR CUT A SHARP EDGE on his buzz. It was probably a good time to return to the Golden Spike, there might even be a craps game going by now for him to showcase his hands, but Davitz retraced his path, waved at the patrol car passing the other way. He'd always heard that the whorehouses in Elko were Nevada's best. Tonight seemed like the perfect time to find out. He returned to the Cartwheel long enough to get directions from a bartender.

Davitz tipped him a silver dollar, made his way to the location where he mistakenly parked his car a block away.

The building itself was disappointing. He had expected something gaudy like white alabaster columns, or a brass railing encircling the yard. What he entered seemed to be four triple wides that formed a natural foyer where three drunk men and a pair of security goons stood around a half-stocked bar.

"Good evening!" a voice lower than his announced from behind. Davitz, surprised, swung hurriedly to face a woman who was a good foot shorter than he expected. "What's your pleasure tonight?"

"Pleasure," he said, feeling foolish.

"We can do that," the madam said. "Let me show you who we have. This is America, you know. Freedom of choice."

Because she too reminded him of Dale Evans, *Could she be the cashier's mother?*, he eschewed a line-up. The thought of conversation seemed suddenly appealing so he asked for someone with a Ph.D.

She returned with a copper-toned redhead no taller than herself who reminded him of a 21 dealer he knew at the Sierra Sage, a small, agoraphobic girl who tried to slit her throat on a break. The woman introduced herself as Dr. Rosalind then led him down one of the halls to the farthest room on the right where she stopped to let him enter first. Davitz paused. He looked at her, saw nothing remarkable, wondered if he'd spoken too hastily.

What he expected was a room full of crushed red velvet, gold flecked wallpaper, hand-carved end tables, billowy lamps, pillows. What he saw wasn't an excess of Neapolitan reds and golds, but a suitable forty-dollar motel room hued in quiet blues and greens: sea colors. The only thing that seemed unusual was the shiny, stainless steel bucket with two washcloths draped over the rim.

"Listen," she said, closing the door behind them, "I hate to be so business-like, but I need you to pay first."

"How much?"

"A hundred for an hour. I don't know if you've been here before, but we don't accept credit cards anymore."

"How much for the night?" Davitz asked impulsively.

She looked at her watch. "Three hundred."

"I'll give you two."

"Two-fifty."

"Bet," Davitz said and peeled from his pocket the three hundred dollar bills, a tenth of his bankroll. Thought Davitz: I'm tithing her.

"Would you like a drink?" she asked.

"A beer would be great," he said. "Bring two."

"I'll just take it out of this." She stuffed the money down her cleavage. "Be right back."

In her absence, he removed his shoes, spat in the sink, scanned the room for surveillance cameras until he heard the doorknob turn. She entered with a bucket similar to the one on the floor but filled with ice and beer. One of them she handed to him. Davitz ran the icy bottle across his forehead before opening it.

"I know you're not a doctor," he told her. "And I'll bet your name isn't really Rosalind."

"You're wrong twice," she said benignly.

"What's your degree in?"

"Anthropology. But the field is flooded. And I don't want to live where the openings are." She sat him down on the bed, sat beside him, began undressing him until she felt him recoil. "Are you shy? she asked. "Would you prefer to leave your clothes on?"

This close, Rosalind looked like no woman Davitz knew, certainly not the 21 dealer *Sally?* whose knife had found her voice box instead of her windpipe, who was soon exiled to a perimeter club that didn't mind the worm-like scar that ran across her throat. Davitz now ran his hands over Rosalind, feeling for scars. He found himself staring at her nipples, stiff and pink. They reminded him of erasers. He withdrew his hands, wondered if she could erase him with these pencil ends.

"So what's your line of work?"

"I'm a craps dealer," he said. "Or was. I'm retired." He allowed Rosalind to finish undressing him. He watched her place his clothes on hangers. He sipped his beer while she removed one of the washcloths from the bucket on the floor. He stared straight ahead while she washed him.

Apparently, Rosalind was already clean. When she was done with him, she set the bucket by the door, returned, began strumming her fingers down his back. Davitz felt the scratch from a ring, grabbed the offending hand. He was angry with himself for not noticing her jewelry. Angry that a decade of watching people's hands, the only part of someone he was ever asked to observe, was so quickly forgotten. Disappointed that it wasn't the engagement ring he had hoped to find.

"Not so rough," Rosalind said.

"Have you ever been married?" Davitz asked.

"Is this an offer?"

"I'm serious."

"Of course I've been married. Who hasn't?"

"Are you married now?"

"No." Rosalind stopped her hands. "That's not something I would do to a guy."

"Do you have kids?"

"No. I can't have children." She laughed, then withdrew her hands altogether. "I certainly chose the right profession, didn't I? I've got the best insurance policy of all." She took a pull from his beer. "It must be exciting to be a dealer."

"I'm not sure it's all that different from what you do," Davitz told her, realizing his words provided little comfort. "We're all tramps anyway. Fidelity means nothing."

"The price of everything, the value of nothing. Oscar Wilde."

"You owe allegiance only to yourself."

"That's crap," Rosalind said. "Allegiance? Fidelity? Listen to you. If fidelity is such a big deal, then why are you here?"

Davitz rested his beer bottle on the nightstand. He was making a mess of all this. He quit talking, saw the bucket by the door, wondered if there were a bucket and washcloth for all the wrong things he'd ever said. He drew her to him. She resisted long enough to shed her negligee and grab a packet from a box inside the bed stand drawer.

He let her do all the work, imagining her to be Sally. The cashier. Hedderly's wife. His waitress. She became just another town he was passing through. He envisioned a white R resting on her hip. Afterward, she took the second washcloth, a pink one, for herself. She told Davitz that he was exquisite.

He smiled weakly, had her bring another pair of beers. This time, she kept one for herself.

"So what's your name?" she asked.

"Hedderly."

"I don't care about that. I mean your first name."

"Tarkio," he said, the name of the Montana border town he'd grown up in. "Tarkio the Sharkio."

"I'm not calling you that."

"Then call me Tark. Or Shark. Shark's my nickname." He told her how Hedderly coined the name. About the various clubs he'd gotten fired from for refusing to kowtow, about Sherwood, about his dismissal from the Diamond Mine for refusing to accept 21 shifts. "21 is skirt work," he told her and raised both of his hands. "You're looking at two of Nevada's best. God made these hands for high limit craps."

"Really?" Rosalind said. "I usually feel a man's hands more than anything else, but I don't remember yours." She gathered his hands and studied one. "You have nice hands," she decided while running a thumb across his manicured nails. "So why don't you want to keep dealing?"

Davitz shrank. What could he tell her? That he was blessed with fast hands and cursed with a faster tongue? That he had run out of fools to suffer? That the decision to deal no longer rested in his own sweet hands but in the hands of these same fools? That wasn't something he was willing to admit, so he told her that he quit for the same reasons she chose not to teach.

Rosalind smiled knowingly. Davitz told her to sleep, that he'd awaken her when he was ready.

"Tonight is an anomaly," Rosalind said. "I'm not used to sleeping on the job."

It bothered him that she could fall so soundly asleep in his presence, but it made his escape easy. Davitz found his clothes, drained the last of his beer, looked at her a final time. "I'm a shark," he whispered to her. To the rising sun. "Sharks never sleep."

AT WELLS, IT OCCURRED TO HIM that if he took 93 North, he could reach his parents' home, the new one he'd never seen, by dinner time. Instead, he took three deep hits off a fresh joint, stayed fixed toward Wendover.

He watched the desert flip-flop so that the pinion pines and the sagebrush looked like the exposed roots of trees growing into the desert, not out of it. It made him feel like a marmot that had scurried down a hole. On the high shelf east of town, the desert righted itself and became an ocean floor. The sagebrush became kelp. The Pequop Mountains, a coral reef. He felt the wind, unusual for this time of day, rock his car in imaginary waves. He saw the desert grit cling to his windshield wipers and side mirror like barnacles on a fish. "I'm a shark," he kept reminding himself. "A shark."

ATOP THE CREST WEST OF TOWN, he beheld the salt flats that ran forever beyond Wendover. It was a longer stretch of land than he had ever seen, and for a moment he thought about driving on, about allowing his two good hands to manipulate something new. There had to be something for him beyond Nevada. Then he caught a glimpse of his disheveled hair and day-old beard and sayonara eyes that hadn't defeated sleep for forty-five hours and figured that any advantage he held ended at the borderline. "Bend over in Wendover," he said to himself in the men's room at the Prima Donna Casino where he rearranged his hair and swallowed five handfuls of water from the sink before making his way out to the main floor.

He was surprised at the activity at the tables. Nine-thirty in the morning and not one dead game. Even the craps table had action although it was apparent from the lack of hoopla which way the dice were running. He examined the faces of the four pit bosses, one of them a woman, but couldn't tell if they were graveyard or day shift. Davitz drew in a breath, tasted his tongue, saw that his hands were shaking. He began walking quickly to the podium, anxious to get there before the four of them dispersed.

"My name is Michael Davitz," he announced. "I'm a craps dealer looking for work. I've spent the last decade dealing in Reno. I'd like to spend the next decade dealing here." He extended his hand. The three men shook it.

"Davitz?" the youngest of them asked. "Why does that name ring a bell?"

Davitz didn't answer.

"What clubs in Reno?" the woman asked.

"You name 'em," he said and instantly wished he hadn't. "Most recently, the Aces Oasis."

"Do you know Dick Stanton?" asked the one Davitz guessed was the shifter.

"No."

"Ed Sherwood?"

"You bet. I could have him fax you a letter of recommendation if that would help." Davitz felt his face flush.

"Have him fax out some bad luck for the players too," the shifter said.

"Let me audition for you," Davitz said. "I can make players bet their front teeth. I'll have your PC back to normal within a month. What are you trying to hold here? Seventeen percent?"

Only the shifter smiled at this. The woman shifted her weight away from Davitz. The young one walked away to the craps table. "Are we hiring?" the shifter asked the other two.

Their hesitance to respond was all Davitz needed. "Watch me," he said. He walked down the pit to the craps table and pushed out the dealer on the busier side. When the dealer attempted to explain which bets belonged to which players, Davitz dismissed him with a wave of the hand. "Got it," he said, and then to the stickman, "What time's the next roll?"

He sensed that the stickman was purposely trying to run him over, not allow him enough time to pay off his bets, but for ten minutes, Davitz held up his end, asking his two money players as he paid their bets whether they wanted to press or parlay their bets. He stymied the boxman as well. Twice, when questioned about a payoff, Davitz broke down the bet to show it was correctly paid. When he finally pushed out, three of the players threw in tips which Davitz tapped on the box in exaggerated thrusts, thanked everyone for playing at the Prima Donna, tucked the tips into his relief's breast pocket.

"Should I go out on the stick?" he asked the shifter, who stood beyond the two pit bosses boxing the game. "Would you like to hear my calls?"

"I think we've seen enough," the shifter said.

"And heard enough," the woman added.

"So do I have a job?"

The shifter tucked his thumb inside the waistline of his pants, ran it from pocket to pocket, looked up with what Davitz took to be regret. "We don't do things the same way they do in Reno," he said. "Different things matter out here."

"You're turning down these hands?" Davitz held them out for everyone to see.

"No," said the shifter. "Not the hands."

Davitz saw the young pit boss squeeze the shoulder of the woman, then stare at him as if he were a lump of flesh. "Fine," Davitz told them. "It's your loss."

"Don't let the door hit you in the ass on your way out," the woman said.

Davitz laughed in disbelief, then extended a hand and formed a C, the half inch gap between his index fingertip and thumb his arrant measure of her, a gesture that prompted the young one to pick up the phone, Davitz guessed, for security.

He retreated slowly, determined to show them that he was leaving on his own terms. Maybe the games were different in Reno, but pit bosses, he decided, were universal. Dead weight. Hillside stones. At the craps table, he paused to watch the dealer he had spelled struggle to come up with the correct payoff, then spill the chips when he attempted to pay off the bet. Just as well, Davitz thought. It was the wrong amount anyway.

Davitz hopped the velvet banister. Again, he pushed out the dealer. "The payoff is eighty-four," Davitz told him. "Here's how you pay it," and showed him the move. He signaled the stickman to send out the dice. He paid the next round of bets, explaining to the rookie when to size into a bet and when to drop cut.

The looks on the other dealers' faces told him security was coming, but Davitz nodded to the stickman to send out the dice. These hands. This game. He wanted to deal just one more roll of the dice. Just one more roll.

SILVER STATE

When Gessler was five, his mother decided it was time he learned how to swim. Bridling at the notion of lessons—why pay for something instinctive?—she carried Gessler in her loving arms to the end of the dock then dropped him into the lake. Momentarily, Gessler struggled. Then sank. Then felt his toes touch the seaweed and soft silt bottom that did not mire him to an underwater grave, but rather, caused him to spring violently to the surface where again he floundered until he determined that no one was watching. Gessler thrashed his way to one of the end posts. Gulping good air, he propelled himself from post to slimy post until he reached shore. Warily, he eyed the back of his mother's summer dress. When he was certain of her indifference, he blew the water out of each nostril and eased himself back into the lake, convincing himself to trust the water.

Still, it's not the pride of accomplishment but naked panic that Gessler summons each time he comes upon unexpected water. His California casino buddies marvel how someone from New Jersey can swim as well as he does, but even now, a good two hundred yards above the Truckee River where he sits on a rock hot enough to melt a diamond, Gessler envisions himself unable to right himself in the waist-high

147

water of the Truckee. Below him, at river's edge, there seems to be some sort of commotion, a dozen people all dressed in white robes, some Gandhifest, but Gessler is too distracted to investigate.

It hasn't been a good week. Both tires on his mountain bike are flat, and the rear tube is too embroidered to take on another patch. The hot water in the shower no longer runs, and the apartment manager seems loath to do anything about it. At the Aces Oasis, the casino manager himself approached Gessler about his flailing hair. "Comb it tonight," he said. "Cut it tomorrow." And now Polly wants him to put in for the bartender training school that's just been posted.

His repeated reminders this morning of his preference for bud, not Budweiser, did little to dissuade her. "You're not consuming drinks; you're serving them. Besides," Polly said, "it's a trade you can take anywhere."

"Like dealing weed?" Gessler asked. "Like pimping?"

Polly examined him fully, a look that always made Gessler feel like he was being frisked. "I don't get you. Or your arrested development," she said, turning away as if Gessler's lack of ambition was contagious. "You're smart. And funny. And incredibly artistic. You could be anything you want." She sighed, for his sake he guessed. "So why don't you want to be more?"

"More what?"

"More anything. What are you going to do, work in slots all your life? You look like my grandmother in that change walker."

"Sorry, not all of us have the cleavage to be a cocktail waitress." A low blow, Gessler knew, bringing to her attention Polly's greatest insecurity, her lack of chest. His repentant bow, perhaps too exaggerated, caused Polly to fling her saucer close enough to make him duck. Her petulance made him laugh, which only made things worse. "Get out! Get out of my house!" she shouted as she reached for another dish.

"Our house," Gessler corrected. "And it's an apartment, not a house."

They've had blowouts before, and Gessler has an SOP. He locates his pipe and stash that he keeps hidden behind the front curtain before going for a bike ride along Mac-Carren Boulevard long enough for her to cool down. Lighting up and lighting out. Nothing better. But this time, it's different and it's not that he's forced to take his car instead of his bike, or that the heat from the rock he's perched on seems to be drawing the marijuana high out of him. Though Polly's big thing is revealment, it pained her to admit that she longs for bigger breasts, pained her more to capitulate to her shifter's suggestion that she wear a Wonderbra underneath her cocktail hostess uniform. "Careful," Gessler warned the first time she donned it for work, "You could poke someone's eye out. Both eyes." By her own admission, she now owns six of these contraptions that pinch her breasts into what look to Gessler, even from his slot station thirty feet away, like two emerging blisters.

In a cluster of nearby sage, Gessler hears a rustling similar to the sound he and Polly heard a month ago while hiking up Peavine Mountain. What Polly thought might be an approaching black bear turned out to be a cow. "It's a swarm of killer beef," Gessler teased, reluctant to admit that the sound had scared him too. He has come to realize that what is discussion to him is argument to her, and that any chance to make a point evaporates after thirty seconds, right after Polly voices her disfavor then quickly adds as the final period to her paragraph, "I don't want to argue with you."

Revealment, he understands, passes only through certain mood channels, for which there is no discernible tide chart. This has been true from the start.

Initially, he had found her bluntness refreshing, that out of the blue she would say things like, "Get that boy some honey for his stinger." Or "I've never dated anyone left-handed." They had seemed like such odd things to say, even stranger than a cocktail hostess stooping to ask out someone from slots, but when Polly accepted on their third date Gessler's invitation to spend the night, just before she acquiesced, she said, "I hope you don't mind women with small breasts." It was the first time he'd received the visual frisk. Then she added, "I'm spending the night here. You're not driving me home." Gessler drew her to him. He couldn't decide which of the two remarks he found more endearing. But this openness has become less attractive now that she expects it from him. Each time he confesses to her things like, "I've never liked the taste of beer," it sounds more apologetic than confiding.

When he hears the sound a second time, more of a scratching noise than a rustle, Gessler stiffly gets to his feet. He walks over to the clump of sage, never taking his eyes off the ground. It's May, the start of rattlesnake season. Gessler examines the half dozen sage bushes, even combs through them with a stick, but finds nothing. Probably a marmot or a chipmunk, he decides. Below him, the diaper people again draw his attention. One of them has waded into the river and is addressing the rest of them who stand along the riverbank in rapt attention. Gessler decides to eavesdrop. He thinks about going back to the car to make sure it's locked, decides that except for his bike gloves and helmet, there's nothing to steal.

The path to the river is a narrow one that alternates between being a dirt trail and a series of small boulders. Gessler is careful about which rocks to traverse. One misstep could send him hurtling down the ravine, or snare and snap a leg. And these are the rocks, the sunny ones, that attract the snakes. Gessler dislikes having to pay this much attention to the sheer act of walking. It's one of the pleasures of being high, distraction. Gessler has never understood people who get high before going out in public. Like half the slot people on his shift who come back so intent from their breaks. Why get stoned then pretend you're not? The joy to him lies in avoiding his own minutiae, not recreating it. That's why his confessions ring more false to him than they must to Polly.

Gessler uses his hands and his feet, crab walking, to negotiate the largest boulder. As soon as he spots a flat surface where the trail picks up again, he begins a controlled slide, leaping free the last few feet. On this final push, his palms scrape first on the rocks, then on the path he has leapfrogged onto. Gessler wishes now he'd thought to go back to the car for his bike gloves. Dust catches in his throat, momentarily gagging him, and as much he detests the idea, Gessler realizes that if someone placed a beer in front of him right now, he'd drink it.

He dusts his hands free of their grit like a dealer leaving a 21 game. That's where Polly is wrong. It's not just serving alcohol that makes Gessler wary to put in for the bartenders' school. Or the fact that upon completion, the casino might jump him to another shift. More than once, he has expressed to anyone within earshot how swing shift suits his metabolism to a T. "I think a person should let the day come to him," he inevitably injects into the conversation. And it isn't sloth, or complacency, which is what Polly thinks. What puts him off about tending bar isn't the idea of serving drinks to drunks, but the recognition that what these people want isn't what they need. They are one more thorny reminder that he doesn't know what he wants, only what he doesn't want. And how can he tell Polly this without her assuming that she must also be on the unwanted side of his ledger.

Once he reaches the knot of cottonwoods, Gessler picks up his pace, almost to a dead run. He cannot see the river from this shelf, but the fecundity of trees and wild grass tells him he is close. Gessler notices a loose shoestring and bends to tie it. He hears a shrill whistle, knows that the marmots have sensed his presence. He cranes, tries to spot the lookout that has stayed behind while the pack retreats to the next hole. Though he is not a joiner, Gessler likes how the marmots operate under duress, one member always willing to risk his safety for the sake of the others, the role of sentinel passed from hole to hole. Gessler mimics the whistle, hoping to assuage their fear. There is no reply.

Why not? Arrested development, Gessler thinks. He rocks in his arms an imaginary child, allows the momentum of his rocking to push him to a sitting position. Arrested development. That's how his connection described his ability to grow such righteous weed, using the term again when he pointed out the silver hairs threading the sticky buds, as if Gessler needed the pitch. Still, it was a positive thing when the bagman said it. Whenever Polly utters those words, it's as if she's learning German. From her, arrested development sounds damning, not desirable, and whenever she accuses him of it, Gessler bristles. It only reinforces his belief that all ambition is suspect.

A month ago, when Polly got on him for blowing his paycheck at a craps table, told him he wasn't holding up his end of the deal, that his days of arrested development were numbered, at least with her, Gessler thought about moving on. As soon as she left for work, he packed his clothes and his bike and gear and wrote a hurried note exonerating her from all blame. He got as far as Soda Springs before turning back. In Truckee, he stopped at the Bar of America and ordered a scotch and water tall, his mother's drink, that he never finished. It was now twilight, not a good time to be pulling off to the shoulder on I-80, but at the border, Gessler spent the last sliver of sunlight staring at the road sign. *Welcome to Nevada*, it said. *The Silver State.* And below: *Recreation Unlimited.* That was it exactly, he decided. Leisure, not purpose, was what gave him hope. Untethered by ambition, anything was possible. Gessler resumed driving, eager to see Polly and to rest his bare feet on warm Nevada sand. Fleeing to California, he knew, would have required a plan.

Gessler now rears back in deference to this recollection. He will try explaining his reluctance to Polly when he returns. No, being a slot change person isn't a forever, but what is?

A chirp that seems painful, not the call of an angry bird, brings Gessler to his feet. He waits until he hears it again then starts down the open trail toward the sound. Gessler can see the river now, and he guesses that he's no more than thirty feet above the throng. At the end of the straightaway, Gessler locates the source of the wailing. Bound in a trap that someone intentionally set in the middle of the trail is the biggest marmot he has ever seen. Even from three yards away, in the jaws of a trap so new its silver sheen glints in the noonday sun, Gessler can make out two exposed pearl leg bones and the mass of ripped, reddened flesh around them.

Gessler wrings his hands, frustrated by his inability to get closer. Each time he makes an attempt, the marmot, its fear of Gessler more pressing than its pain, wriggles in futile flight, cutting its trapped hind leg further to the bone. Gessler sits in the middle of the path at a distance he hopes is non-threatening. He watches the marmot, fatter than a football, watching him, wonders how to go about disengaging the trap in a way that will not cause the marmot more suffering or cause himself to get bit.

He never gets the chance. Just as he's about to rise and free the poor thing, to hell with injury, the marmot sighs, expelling air like a flat tire, then closes its eyes forever.

Gessler approaches the marmot, sees the swelling motion in its belly, understands now its extended size—and its fear. Though he understands too that there is a delicate cycle of life in the desert, Gessler cannot bring himself to leave things as they are. In a small clearing where the ground seems soft, Gessler uses an edged rock to dig two holes, one for the marmot, one for the trap. The slippery blood makes freeing the animal difficult, so Gessler works slowly. Afterwards, he uses a tumbleweed to erase all evidence just in case the bastard comes back for his trap. Then Gessler pauses. He feels stupid. It was just an animal, one of ten million. Still, it seems to Gessler there should remain some sign of a life.

Conflicted about washing away the evidential blood and grime, Gessler walks slowly toward the river, palms angled as if they are also two arms of a trap. He is glad that he is no longer high and decides that when he gets home, if Polly is there, he will tell her he is sorry, that perhaps it is time to shift gears, that he intends to apply for the bartenders' school. That he would be grateful if she would use her juice with the beverage manager to get him an interview. No, it isn't what he wants, it's what she wants, but if she feels remorse, feels that she has browbeaten him into applying, he will reassure her. "You're right," he'll tell her. "I *am* smart. I'm just not smart about myself." For the good of the pack, he will whistle her warning.

Gessler pauses at the riverbank then resolutely wades into the Truckee up to his knees, but before he can cleanse his sullied hands, he hears the beckoning of the faithful fifty feet away. "Brother, will you join us?" their leader shouts. "Will you receive the word?" Gessler feels the current, something, brush his leg, but his dismay gives way to the coolness of the water. Thinks Gessler: how good this feels. He searches the river around him for trout. He sees that he has kept his palms skyward the entire time, and that the fifteen swaddled souls, some already doused in sacrament, are regarding him with what Gessler believes is reverence. One of them points at him a silver ankh that shimmers like the river. Silver, Gessler knows, the reward for second best.

ACKNOWLEDGMENTS

Gratefully acknowledged are the following publications, where stories first appeared in earlier versions:

"This Wretched Conscience" appeared in *The RavensPerch Literary Magazine.*

"Jackpots Only" first appeared in *The Carolina Quarterly* and more recently in *Muddy Backroads: Stories from off the Beaten Path* (Madville 2022).

"Suits and Bodies" appeared in *Berkeley Fiction Review.*

"Bank Job" appeared in *Talking River Review.*

"True Odds" appeared in *Green Mountains Review.*

"Photo Op" appeared in *Jabberwock Review.*

"Dead Bob's Story" appeared in *The Nebraska Review.*

"Sand Shark" appeared in *South Dakota Review.*

* * *

I haven't found many advantages to aging, but here's one, a heightened sense of gratitude, which makes this page an easy one to craft. First and foremost, I want to thank the team at Cornerstone Press: on the writing end, Director and Publisher, Dr. Ross Tangedal, and Senior Editor extraordinaire, Brett Hill; on the publicity and promotion end, Ava Willett and Sophie McPherson. I want to thank Corrina Wycoff, Michael Czyzniejewski, Matthew Sullivan, Christopher Coake, Peter Donahue, and Barry Kitterman, some of whom I've never met in person, all of whom, while not lacking things to do, took the time to read this collection and respond to it positively. I want to thank Derek Sheffield, whose poetry has found the national attention it deserves while he continues to advocate for others, particularly those of us in the Pacific Northwest.

In posthumous praise, I want to laud my high school English teacher, Ms. Lauren Pipp. Ditto Mike and Barbara Land, former professors at the University of Nevada, Reno, who got across the notion that perhaps I'd be better served writing about the casino life than merely living it. I want to acknowledge Montana icons Bill Kittredge, Jim Crumley, and Bryan DiSalvatore, all of whom helped me glimpse Reno and its casinos from an honest distance. If there's a better town than Missoula for writers and poets to gather, I don't know it. Two from that era who can and should learn my gratitude are Earl Ganz, and Gerry Brenner, who, when I was a graduate student, became my mentor, tormentor when necessary, and role model for the college classroom educator I aspired to become.

I want to thank John Range, Laureen Fong-Frydendal, and Jimi Frydendal, Reno roommates who provided mooring beyond the casino air curtains. Rick Bohm too, whose passing still haunts me. And though I'm not sure why, Steve Kuriscak, my craps school instructor, whose sage advice, "Don't be too good the first time, or they'll expect it every time," has proffered a multitude of applications.

Lastly, there's Joanne Lisosky, one of the first female craps dealers, who escaped with me to other places. I cannot imagine sharing my life with anyone else.

MICHAEL DARCHER, a former casino dealer and gaming instructor, taught English for a quarter century at Pierce College in Washington state. His stories have appeared in *High Plains Literary Review, The Carolina Quarterly, Green Mountains Review, Zone 3, Berkeley Fiction Review, The Nebraska Review,* and elsewhere. Michael resides above Commencement Bay in Tacoma with his wife, Joanne.

Milton Keynes UK
Ingram Content Group UK Ltd.
UKHW030745071024
449371UK00006B/529

9 781960 329455